Geoffrey Rose's second novel is an exciting account of a young Englishman's attempt to evade capture and death in the Russian winter of 1917, and to reach Archangel where a British ship awaits him. He is a spy, caught up in the convulsions of the collapsing Russian State. Despite the precise detail, there is a dream-like quality about his plight in the endless, killing snow, in wolf-haunted forests, in the distances that never seem to lessen. Sometimes, and unexpectedly, hands reach out to aid and succour. Fortune can be a grimace or a grin – and sometimes is murderous. This gripping novel is an experience for the fugitive and reader, with incidents now sharp, now fading, like expelled breath in a frozen landscape.

'The hazy, dream-like atmosphere of unreality surrounding such an adventure recollected long afterwards is well conveyed.' *Irish Times*

Also by Geoffrey Rose in Panther Books

Nobody on the Road

Geoffrey Rose

A Clear Road to Archangel

Panther

Granada Publishing Limited
Published in 1975 by Panther Books Ltd
Frogmore, St Albans, Herts AL2 2NF

First published in Great Britain by
Macmillan London Ltd 1973
Copyright © Geoffrey Rose 1973
Made and printed in Great Britain by
Richard Clay (The Chaucer Press) Ltd
Bungay, Suffolk
Set in Monotype Plantin

PART ONE

I

There was snow. There was not more of it visible to me than I'd seen in England, but a sense of the infinitude I couldn't see, going on for ever across the steppes, made of that Russian snow a different element.

There was a bridge. I had been running a long time, halting only to sob for breath, but the bridge is the first thing I recall seeing, so dawn must have come as I reached it. Though the night had never been truly dark, because of the snow glare.

As soon as I saw the bridge, redundant on a frozen river, I saw in the middle distance beyond it a line of horsemen, stationed at regular intervals and motionless, silhouetted against the first light. Part of my training, an immeasurable time ago, had been the identification of foreign soldiers by silhouette only. Characteristically, since it was the least useful part of my training, I had become quite good at it, and now I had no difficulty in identifying these as Caucasian cavalry. Very cold they must be, not moving. They didn't need to move. With two other lines they formed a triangle. (Why a triangle? Why not a circle? I don't know why. I knew only that it was so, as I knew a lot else of their tactical and strategical habits. It would be a triangle, with a command-post at its apex and a subordinate post, actually only a relay station, at each of the other two angles.) They had only to wait. Our chance of getting through was negligible. They would take us alive; those were the orders. Sooner or later two sides of that triangle would sweep slowly inward, the third keeping station to watch.

The question was, at which point of the formation had I most chance of breaking through? Or rather, to word it realistically, least risk of being caught? There was no question of cover once that sweep began – rivers frozen, farms ready tinder, peasantry intimidated. Seen with a backward glance, the fortress from which I had last night escaped, that loomed still massive and purple, gained an almost paternal appearance in contrast to these new terrors.

Of course, I might have been spotted already. Prolonging the business would amuse them. I wondered where Mikhail was. They might simply hold their triangle about us, like a mystic symbol about the damned, moving with us, never nearer never farther, letting the knives of winter do their work for them. But of course they wouldn't do that. I was getting confused. We must be recaptured, alive, at once, so Captain S might resume his 'conversations' with us. I must beware of mental confusion. Clarity of thought was the only equipment I had for this escape, and the manner of my recent life had not improved it. The ice of the scene was puzzling my eyes, glittering like false diamonds under the low sun. Well, I could rest now – must rest, since the sun was up – and recuperate mind and body.

By 'conversation' Captain S meant interrogation under torture; and even the beginning of it had been enough to make me prefer any other hardship. I did not speak Russian – otherwise poor Mikhail would not have been lying out in this graveyard with me – but Captain S spoke English. Captain S had read English authors, and would discuss the works of Dickens with me in the necessary intervals of 'conversation'. I did not like discussing the works of Dickens with Captain S; I did not want those books spoiled for me by associations of pain, fear, despair; yet they were something familiar to grip in the nightmare landscape where the Captain compelled me to walk. And the despair can't have been absolute while I looked forward to a time when I should read them again.

Why did the Captain, whom a month before I'd never heard of and fifty years later can still not forget, seek the

8

pleasure of my conversation so persistently? Well, you see, it was felt that I knew rather more of the movements of the army and the intentions of its High Command than a foreigner ought. Especially, as he kept pointing out with sweet reasonableness, a foreign civilian. He implied that had I been a soldier he could almost have forgiven me, but as it was — He never uttered the word 'spy', but it hung in the air. I couldn't repudiate it with any show of indignation, since it was right. Nor, of course, could I accept it. Nor would I say who had sent me. Nor would I say what I knew. An accumulation of reticences which inhibited the conversation. He found me, as my friends did, taciturn to a fault. 'Especially in time of war,' as he kept saying.

It wasn't really time of war for him. Russia had collapsed out of it. But he may have been justified in thinking the resultant chaos worse than war. To say I knew the movements of the Russian army and the intentions of its High Command better than they did themselves, is not to claim any unusual degree of perspicacity, and is probably to credit them with what they no longer had. But the British Government wanted to be assured that our ally, who had looked as lifelike as a well-made snowman and proved about as forceful, having melted from our side would not materialise on the other. I suppose they still believed the myth of his power. I don't know that I should have harmed anybody by confessing to Captain S the precise nature of my errand and conclusions, but I had only my orders to guide me. As he had his. I wonder whether I might have liked him, but for his orders. I rather think without them he would not have existed, being purely an embodiment and execution of them. Probably he had been ordered to read Dickens.

I thought things like these lying in the lee of the bridge, blinking from my eyes the flakes of snow which never left off falling for long. Snow advanced across the land, undeterred by river and undeflected by forest, as the Russian army had ben expected to advance. But the army was demoralised, disintegrated. In this area probably no more remained of it than enough men to implant this grey triangle on the snow.

Perversely, the falling flakes had the effect lacking in the fallen mass: they reminded me of a Christmas card. Christmas was still to come, I believed. English Christmas, that is. The Russian one was different. At the fortress they had been careful to keep us ignorant of the date – part of an attempt to remove all mental landmarks, I suppose – but I thought English Christmas was still to come. I fixed my eyes on the nearest flakes, and strove even among them to isolate and trace the fall of one or two. If I looked beyond them the infinite vistas and vortices dizzied me until they seemed to be going all ways, even upward, and I felt sick.

The line of cavalry sat motionless yet, bar little fidgetings of horse and man – two beasts made one for practical purposes. Soon the men would have a white uniform instead of grey, and would stand or move unseen in the white world. I wondered what special faith or subjection kept them at their posts when every instinct must bid them desert. Most of the army had deserted. These must be picked men. I wondered what they thought of me. I pursued these speculations with some effort – to stay awake, to stay clear-headed, and above all to keep my mind off a prospect as dizzying and dangerous as that of the myriad flakes. Because, of course, I too was receiving a white uniform, just as my hunters were: and their eyes, like mine, were being irritated and blinded by the impact and mere sight of snow. And when we all began to move, the odds would be slightly better in my case – who had only to get beyond one of those lines, anywhere beyond it – and slightly worse in theirs, who had to locate and converge on a precise point. Say my chance of getting through was raised from point one per cent to point two.

I must keep my mind off this possibility. Even if I got out of the triangle, there was an eternity of travelling, deception, exhaustion, starvation, to face beyond. An infinity of track-less plain, blocked roads, succourless forest. My chance of survival there was less than my chance of escape here. I must think in inches and minutes, or the vastness of the prospect would bewilder me. At least I had my warmest prison cloth-ing on. We had waited for the outdoor exercise time to escape in, for that reason. To distract myself from mirages, I tried to imagine myself in the cavalry commander's place. Such efforts of sympathy were part of my work. The General himself would be in command, issued from the inmost box of the many-boxed fortress to direct this operation on which his subsequent career might depend. I had never seen him, though I believe he had witnessed some of the 'conversa-tions'. To take a prisoner is more difficult than to leave a corpse. He would see how the falling snow helped me and hindered him. He would sit in his command-post, slow and stolid – I reckoned the volatile commanders were dead or vanished – pondering our chances. I could picture the kind of stove he was sitting by, the kind of glass he was drinking tea from – I reckoned the tippling commanders had gone with the volatile. He would see what I could see – that the snow was falling more thickly, that visibility was shorten-ing. He must decide which of us should move first on this chess-board from which all squares were obliterated, where one pawn stood hemmed by many knights. And he must decide soon, while he could still see the moves. Ideally he needed drag-nets of rope or wire, unbroken for the length of each line and attached to each horse by two bars which would keep the net from the hind hoofs. Not infallible, but two such nets drawn swiftly together across open level ground ought to entangle me. Luckily, such nets are not standard items of equipment, and I doubted whether he had expected my escape. I hadn't myself until suddenly driven to it by the pressure of the Captain's interrogation.

At first sight it was amazing that I'd been let escape. But on second thoughts it was explicable. The Russian military temperament had an immense power of concentration on the immediate task and a corresponding tendency to neglect related ones. The Captain, and behind him the General and the High Command, all obedient to this temperamental law, had exerted their strength in the task of interrogating me and left themselves not quite enough for that of holding me prisoner. Their bias gave them an image so vivid of one aspect of a person or situation that it blinded them to all others. I had appeared to them so clearly a man to be questioned that they scarcely saw me as a man who must be guarded.

I wondered how this failing might act in the General's mind now. How would he deploy his knights? He must decide soon, and convey his decision to the two subordinate command-posts for relay to the ranks. Normally semaphore would be used for the first stage of the message, but the snow mocked that. He might have had time to set up electric telegraph link between the posts, but it was unlikely, and anyway the military telegraph was notorious for breaking down. More probably couriers would be sent, one to each secondary commander, who in turn would send his own courier to the ranks. And all that would take time. It would be quicker if the General's couriers gave his orders as they rode down the lines, but that was not the way of it. Correct etiquette must be maintained – more than ever now, when only it held together the remnant of the army. So, continuing my impersonation of my adversary, I reasoned. The couriers, aides-de-camp, would be of better birth, if not higher rank, than the subordinate commanders to whom they carried the General's decision. They would not deign to address the common soldiers – probably couldn't, speaking only fashionable French. And the subordinate commanders for their part would be jealous of the right to issue orders to their men directly or by their own intermediaries. It would all be done to rule. It would take time. And the passing minutes were as much my friends as the falling flakes. I must see how best to use their help. How does a line of cavalry advance? I asked myself. And would this weather make any difference to the customary manner? These weren't academic questions. Cavalry tends to bunch as it advances, perhaps because of a nervous disposition in man and horse to seek the fellowship of their kind in face of the enemy. If the two approaching lines were going to bunch this morning, I must move now – try to penetrate one line while it still stood or to judge and reach that point where the shrinkage would occur between the moving lines and the apex or base of the triangle. But would snow change the habit? Recalling my own little riding, I thought it would. Dazzled by snow and fearful of collision, they would tend to widen the intervals between themselves. On balance, I'd better wait. If I was wrong, flailing hoofs wouldn't do me much good; but the thought of crawling toward a line of men whose whole attention was still in vigilance was no more inviting to my cowardice.

My guesses were right in one particular at least. There went the General's courier, galloping the length of the line I could see. The other sides of the triangle were hidden from me, as were the extremities of this line, by rising ground and some farm buildings and trees, so I must judge the condition of the whole by the fragment visible. How would the order to advance be given? By trumpet call, or by an agreed time? The call was safer. Army watches were like the Army telegraph. I wondered whether Captain S was among my huntsmen. The possibility was more repugnant to me than all others. I should hate to be plucked from the snow by his manicured hands.

Despite my precautions, the fall of flakes was confusing me. I fancied a music in it, made by the flakes. I must have been dreaming of a Christmas toy – an elaborate card, perhaps – in which a representation of falling snow was somehow linked with a musical box. And there seemed to be a woman in a horse-drawn sleigh, too. No women here. Nor sleighs, which were for the moment infinitely more desirable. It had been at the Rector's I'd seen that card. At a Christmas party at Mr Prout's. The same Christmas he had puzzled us all with mnemonic tricks and turned my interest that way and so set my feet towards Russia. It was Mr Prout's doing that I was here. I might, to my peril, have pursued Mr Prout further through a diminishing perspective of years and album leaves and his Crimean memories (he had been a chaplain), falling into that sleep the snow bestows before death, which is its most insidious weapon; but I was recalled by the sound of guns. German guns, they must be. The Russians hadn't any to speak of. Hadn't any to do more with than speak of, that is. But this bombardment was not a heavenly intervention on my behalf. The front, though getting farther back each day, was still too distant for its activity to interrupt our present business. A few heads turned, and that was all.

I wondered what Mikhail was thinking. His would be an animal's instinctive response to danger, not my articulate appraisal. Probably his was better. I wished we were together. But it had been wise to part, to split the pursuit. The direction of the courier had confirmed my guess that the apex of the triangle was away to my left, nearer the fortress, the triangle opening out to engorge the farther country; but I didn't know whether Mikhail lay within its jaws.

The General's courier returned along the line. In a moment he would be followed by another, bearing the orders to the men. This second was slower to appear than I had expected; and when he did, it was not in the way I had expected. He was stopping at each man, giving him individual orders – no, giving him some thing. A club or baton. No, a torch. The first man I could see of the line had lit his. It blazed bravely, the flame streaming on the wind like a pennon. It must be soaked in some damp-defying chemical, for it was not hindered by the falling snow. Now

14

several were alight, beautiful in the morning. Were they to help the men see, or to set fire to what scant cover the ground offered? I should know soon.

To lie still was difficult with so many enemies so near planning my capture. But waiting was my reasoned choice. I couldn't plan further. When the advance began I must do what circumstance permitted or dictated. I glanced to right and left where the frozen course of the river was still distinguished from the ground on either bank, though it wouldn't be much longer, the snow covering both impartially. Had the river been flowing I might have swum to freedom; but, like my luck, it was frozen. And a skater would be a remarked figure in that region. The only unremarkable figure there this morning would be a horseman. Thinking so, I suddenly formulated what I had been conscious of for some time – that the smell of horses was stronger than the distant cavalry could account for in that antiseptic air. One of those farm buildings just behind me must be a stable. Only cart horses, but still— Had I time? I cursed myself for wasting so much, and could hardly discipline myself to crawl instead of running toward the buildings.

Once concealed by them I stood, and fell instantly on the iced cobbles of the yard. Nobody in sight. Probably they were watching the soldiers. In the stable a man was shifting straw. I knew no accent of threat or plea to sound to him. Instead I snarled – literally, baring my teeth – as an animal does faced by one of a strange species. And he cowered against a wall. Those people had long practice in cowering. Maybe I was a more terrifying sight than I knew. Next minute I was mounted. Not quite as I could have wished, but mounted. I thumped the horse's sturdy flanks with my legs – he was better fed than his keeper – and murmured coaxing words at his ear, and he lumbered obediently from the stable. The farm hand showed no wish to follow me, but I bolted the door on him to make sure. I had lost some of my snowy coat in the warmth of the stable, and that was as important to me as a horse, but it was soon replaced. I held the horse in the cover of the buildings while I scanned the scene.

My new point-of-view was disturbing at first; having adjusted to it I saw, through bigger, faster flakes, that the line of cavalry had not moved. Even as I watched, a trumpet call shivered the morning, breaking the spell which had held it motionless. The pennants of flame streamed longer as the line slowly advanced. It was done in silence, the snow muffling the fall of hoofs, so that after the clarion which was either my summons to liberty or the trump of doom for me, if you had listened with eyes shut you would not have suspected any movement. Not at first. Then a low rhythmic murmur was heard. The Cossacks were singing as they rode. Or praying perhaps. I waited in that frozen farmyard – I believe I could draw it in detail even now – dreading that somebody of the house would come on me, dreading that the man I had imprisoned would start to make a row, and above all watching. Watching the line approach so I could judge the moment when the line behind me, still hidden from me by the buildings and the trees beyond, would reach the farm; so I could judge the earliest moment when it was just possible that I, emerging from the farmyard and advancing toward my advancing foes, might be an eager comrade of the opposite line. Imagine trying to judge what a man behind you is doing by watching his reflection in a mirror, and you'll have some feel of the thing. Except that I'd no guarantee I was watching a true reflection, since I didn't know whether I stood mid-way between the lines. A noise in the farmyard out of sight – more than farm people would make, I thought. I must assume it was made by the other line. I urged my horse forward.

He could match at his utmost the pace to which the cavalry horses were being restrained, and at a glance he wasn't much different from them, all being shaggy with snow. My lack of a hat marked me from the other riders. At that amble it could scarcely have fallen off, but perhaps the point would be overlooked in the excitement. Anyway, I couldn't help it. Forward. The faces of my hunters were only a few yards from me, distinctly foreign even under the mask of snow. I could see the breath rise from their mouths as they maintained that strange humming. I began to sing myself. 'Onward, Christian soldiers' was all I could think of – hugely inappropriate, but generating some of the encouragement I needed. I saw their arms raised stiffly to hold the torches aloft as in a ritual. Lack of a torch would surely betray me. I remembered seeing faggots of wood in the farmyard. I could have taken one, but my wits hadn't been working widely enough, and I only wasted energy by useless regret. Anyway, I was passing through the line of Cossacks. The fellow passing on my right looked at me. So far as I could read his face, I thought he saw something wrong in my appearance, but he only stared. Probably there was no regulation form for voicing his doubts, and nobody at hand to voice them to. I held on; still at an amble, unable to go faster even had I dared, and expecting every minute to hear cries, to feel hands laid on me.

I didn't know how the operation was to continue. Possibly the two lines were to halt, having met. Well, I wasn't halting. I could only trust that the officers were a long way off and that nobody else was going to act on his initiative. I held on, and glancing sideways saw that the line behind me was doing the same. I urged my horse to his best speed, fearful of scrutiny if I dropped back. I wondered what the man who had spotted me was doing. I prayed he was thinking about it very slowly, and mindful of the punishments visited on rash action. Glancing back, I saw flame rising from somewhere beyond the farm. I saw too that some of the men I led had no torches, presumably having expended them in the firing; so that was all right. I reckoned we were to take the stations quitted by the other line and there await further orders. But I mustn't wait. Though they rode forgetful of their neighbours, once halted they would immediately notice a stranger where an acquaintance had been. When we reached our new station I must promote myself to the rank of courier and without pause head toward the far corner of the triangle, but veering gently away from the line so that though the men saw me go the command-post should never see me arrive. Now I was riding – riding! – over the bridge where so lately I had crouched. I glanced down, almost expecting to see myself there, so improbable did my change of role seem. The man on either side of me stopped to see that no fugitive hid below.

Judging myself to be where the other line had stood, I turned my horse's head and urged him south, ostensibly toward the secondary command-post. The Cossacks had halted, as I'd expected, and turned to face inward again. Slowly – we couldn't do better than slow – I rode behind their backs. A few turned their heads to watch me as I passed; I betrayed no awareness of them and no man hindered me. The private soldier inhabits a narrow universe, suffering mutely the incursion into it of forces mysteriously benevolent or mysteriously punitive. Heads turned at my passage as heads had turned at the opening of the artillery fire – which still continued – and with as little thought of being called on to do anything about it. Only a courier would ride alone that way; therefore anyone riding alone that way must be a courier. Besides, they had been told to look for a man on foot. A man on horseback, however strange, was not in their terms of reference. Almost gaily, I turned away from the line of Cossacks, letting curtains of snow fall between us.

II

And suddenly I was terribly alone. I felt like the first man on earth, with limitless bewilderment for his lot, except that I felt more like the last man on earth. The wish to get out had filled my mind. Now I was out, the further difficulties loomed so large and indefinite that I wished it undone and myself back again. This is a morbid state of mind which the more thoughtful kind of captivity is aimed to produce. But they hadn't reckoned on my having a horse. He served me as a cat or dog does other solitary folk : he saved my sanity. I had another creature to address and I had transport. Not fast, but at least he kept my feet off the ground. And that was well, since my boots were in bad repair, held together by strips of sacking.

On the debit side, I had no weapon, no food or drink, no map or compass, no notion of where I was – for I'd been brought to the fortress at night, by train – and no command of the language. They had confiscated even my watch. And I didn't know the names of six people in Russia. I knew the names of five. Mikhail and four others – precisely the four whom I must not approach in my trouble for fear of leading the secret police to them. Such as it was, the organisation of my mission was geared to helping me get information, and not at all to saving my skin. I was a shot in the dark, and could not hope to be retrieved if I went astray. Well, luck had been with me so far this morning; I might have struck a vein of it. At least I was trying, moving, instead of help-less under the attentions of Captain S.

Thinking of him reminded me that I did know a sixth name in Russia. (Not his. I didn't reckon him. Disdain as much as discretion gives him only an initial.) He had spoken of a countess, in such phrases as, 'You're as bad as the Countess', 'The Countess might sympathise with your attitude'; but whether she was a person or a proverb, and if a person, alive or dead, and if alive, young or old, I had no means of knowing. She might be wholly the Captain's fiction, devised to tantalise me, for he smilingly refused to answer any question about her; and in effect, anyway, she was little better than a fiction to me, I not knowing where she was nor where I was myself. Sometimes I pictured her young, wrapped in furs, sometimes old, nearly a cadaver, but whatever she was, she was my only light in the whole of dark Russia, and toward the idea of her I directed my flagging thoughts.

But that didn't answer the question of where to go now. I wondered whether I should aim for the railway or avoid it. Since the Tsar's abdication in the spring, and indeed since long before, the country had been disrupted by labour strikes, so probably the railway was a thing to be neither hoped for nor feared, but only so many miles of dead iron. I had been put ashore from a warship at Archangel. If I returned there I should be picked up again. But my chance of reaching Archangel was about as good as my chance of reaching heaven – of which, quite deceptively, its name reminds one. All I knew was that it was in the north, and I turned my horse that way, more as a gesture to encourage myself than as a hopeful action.

I must reduce my thinking to a scale of inches and minutes, as I did before breaking out of the trap. To anticipate reaching Archangel was insane. To anticipate reaching tomorrow was scarcely better. If I could last, well and free, until nightfall, I should have won a great victory, the only victory I should look for at this moment. By nightfall at latest I must find food and shelter for the horse and me. Without them we might die. And this must be done without encountering other men. Nominally, Britain and Russia were allies still, but I wasn't in uniform. And the British authorities would not own me in the event of my failure; I had been warned of that. Nobody loves a spy. And into the bargain I was a horse-thief now.

And there were other reasons for shunning my fellows. The country was full of wanderers – deserters, many of them – their purposes not always friendly. Captain S had said, 'Wait till the others get hold of you! They're not gentlemen. They lack our refinement. We can't lodge you for ever, much as I should like to continue our literary discussions. We haven't enough for ourselves. When you have answered my questions – and you will answer them – we shall let you go. And inevitably you will fall into the hands of the others. Then you will appreciate my restraint. And when they let you go, you will not be good for very much. You will become one of those pathetic, nearly mystic, derelicts our land abounds in.' I didn't know who these 'others' were – they might be more devices of his imagination – but the picture strengthened my resolve to avoid mankind.

Going north was risky, in that it took me toward the fortress, but 'a miss is as good as a mile' – and was better in this instance, perhaps, since they would look for me far rather than near. Thus I could turn the horse's slowness to advantage. And in this weather you might pass your best friend at two yards without knowing, so it wasn't unrealistic to hope that I might pass my worst enemies at a hundred.

A wind was rising, blowing the snow at us in flurries which made my horse shift his head from side to side, though he kept his given way steadily. In lulls of the wind I could hear that the German barrage at the front continued. I wondered whether the General had satisfied himself yet that his trap was empty. (I hoped it was. I hoped Mikhail wasn't in it.) I wondered whether the farm-hand had told his story yet, or invented a better one. They were a great race for inventing stories, those peasants; though in a land full of princes and wolves invention seemed superfluous. I might get provisions as I'd got a horse, but that trick couldn't be counted on to work twice. The next fellow might be of sturdier stuff, and I was in no condition for a struggle. 'No, old chap,' I said to the horse. 'Any food we get must be left out like cream for the fairies – with no people by.' My voice sounded odd and I got a mouthful of snow, so I didn't speak again.

Instead I thought of the General. I mustn't stop thinking of him simply because I was out of the trap. He wouldn't have stopped thinking of me. Quite the contrary. I had run off with his chance of favour and promotion, leaving in its place a good chance of disgrace and punishment. Picturing himself stripped of his rank, sent to Siberia, shot even, he would have me very much in mind – exclusively, I might say without immodesty; and it behoved me to give him first place in mine, rather than be talking to horses. The trap proving empty, its human components would be dispersed, at speed, to search. He would have used at first all the men available. They couldn't form a larger trap effectively, so now they must search. How? Outward from their first positions, or returning to them from a distance?

I was hungry. I had missed two meals, supper and breakfast; and though the prison food was scant, lack of it was telling on me. I remembered going to the National Gallery in London with a cousin, a girl, ages ago when I was still at school, and seeing among hundreds of others that bored me horribly a painting of a ship in a snow storm, where the snow was depicted as making spiral cones. I'd thought it an effective trick. Now I saw that the painter was more observant and less inventive than I'd supposed. The snow did indeed make spiral cones – a whole system, or chaos, of them, filling the world. Of some the points and of others the open ends were nearest me, but all maleficent, all aimed at me like weapons or set for me like traps, and moaning and screaming as the wind marshalled them.

It's hard to believe in other lives concurrent with one's own yet very different. That cousin, for instance. To the best of my knowledge she was alive and well in England. At this moment she was breathing, moving, laughing, choosing presents in a shop perhaps. But I couldn't believe in her existence. England itself seemed incredible. Nothing existed but danger and this system of snowy spirals. Nobody lived but me. Gloria, the General, Captain S, Mr Prout who was dead, the Countess who perhaps had never been alive – on the perimeter of the storm they had an equal and insubstantial footing; but here within the storm was no reality other than me and the horse under me and the snow on my face.

On. Still the wind rose and fell; still the guns sounded; still the horse went forward steadily, turning his head from the flakes as he would turn it from flies in summer. And time passed. That too was hard to believe, nothing marking its passage. The sun was hidden. The landscape, without feature, offered no evidence of our progress. We might have been motionless, only the snow moving. Equally we might have been traversing leagues. On.

If I had found myself at the gates of the fortress, I can't say that I would not have sought admittance. In my exhaustion I might have embraced any alternative to the nihilism of the snow. But it didn't happen that way. I saw neither the fortress nor any of its garrison all that day, and we were still moving in what I prayed was a northward line (I'd heard of men lost in deserts walking in circles) when the sky darkened. My little victory was achieved; I had remained free and well until nightfall. But I had failed to find either food or shelter. We – I used the term then, too, for it made the business seem less solitary – had halted several times to rest and had tried to quench our thirst with snow, but we had seen no sign of habitation.

Now darkness was complete. The gunfire had stopped some time before, having brought final darkness to many no doubt, and the snow had stopped. Even the wind had died. I had grown accustomed to these sounds, as you do to the sound of your pulse on a sleepless night, and their cessation

23

was alarming. Now I could hear only the horse's laboured breathing and the soft sound of his faltering hoofs. But still he kept a straight path, however weakly, and was an example and a reproach to me in my waverings of hope and intent.

But the darkness wasn't complete. Away on my left was a red glare. I couldn't identify it, but it suggested the presence, or at least the work, of people. Despite my good resolution, drawn by the thought of warmth I turned toward the glare. It's easy on the insensible page to blame myself, for paper cannot reproduce the cold. I haven't spoken of the cold. So basic a condition of life goes without saying. Since words can't register it, let me say merely it was like to prove for both of us more a cause of death than a condition of life if much prolonged. We could muster no speed to warm us, you see. Without the snow, my brave horse's best pace would have been little better than a walk. With the snow, it was distinctly worse. I don't know whether he was normally worked at all in winter. Certainly by this hour, when, incredibly, the temperature dropped still lower, he would have been snug indoors. His unquestioning patience was noble and fatuous. A stranger leaping on his back, he would go on to the end of earth and time, or until he dropped, because he believed it to be the prescribed lot of a horse.

So I turned toward the glare which flawed the darkness. Nor was the silence absolute now. From far away I heard a cry, at once evil and hopeless, which I recognised as that of a wolf. My horse, too, knew it, and started and shivered. A knowledge of wolves was instinctive in his mind, no doubt. I urged him to go faster, though he needed no urging, and kept my hearing alert for a nearer repetition of that disquieting cry, or for the reply to it of others, but none came. Perhaps it was a purely ritual utterance; perhaps wolves greet the dark as cocks do the dawn; but you can understand that I saw the eyes of countless imaginary wolves shining on either side of us.

We pressed on toward the glare. It was the first visible goal I'd had to aim at since my country-dance with the Cossacks, and that circumstance alone was cheering. As we approached I saw that the glare was flickering, almost certainly that of a man-made fire, and that it projected intermittently and jerkily on the night, like a bad cinematograph, the dark shape of a building, a house or hut. At the same time I heard voices, raised violently in dispute or song, or both maybe, and at that sound, more threatening to me than the wolf-cry, even I in my headlong rush to warmth had the sense to halt.

I could see now that the building was a low one, raised from the ground and with a verandah about it. The fire seemed to be inside, or possibly in front of it. I couldn't see the people. A whinnying told me that horses were near, and that they'd sensed the presence of my own horse. At the sound, the song or argument stopped abruptly. I wheeled about – only to find myself confronted at a few yards by three figures, stolen upon me as silently as wraiths. I don't know whether they were returning from an expedition or were sentries who had seen my approach. Anyway, there they stood, three soldiers with rifles pointed. Given another kind of horse I would have ridden at them, but my brave fellow wasn't built for tricks like that. As I stood, they advanced, more unsteadily than the snow and their long coats accounted for. They were somewhat drunk, I thought; but that was reason to be cautious rather than bold. Their rifles might not be loaded – I should be surprised if they were, knowing the state of supplies – but it wasn't a chance to gamble on.

They laid hands on me, seeming as surprised as I by our encounter, and pulled me from my horse, more clumsily than roughly. At least they weren't Cossacks, but infantrymen. They marched me toward the hut, where a crowd of soldiers had appeared to see what was happening. I saw by the motley character of the group and by their unkempt condition that I had not blundered on a garrison. These were deserters. I saw too that the building was a railway station. What I'd mistaken for a verandah was the platform, and below it lines were visible where the snow had been shovelled or trodden. Planks had been torn from the platform to make a fire inside the waiting-room – it was really only that, the place being a halt rather than a station – and the room was very hot, despite the door's standing open, and full of smoke and the fumes of spirits. My three captors experienced more difficulty than I in walking the little way to the platform and mounting it. The rest crowded round, staring at me, talking excitedly, plucking at my clothes, but neither helping nor hindering the work of getting me inside. I spent those minutes furiously planning what I should do. My few words of Russian were useless. English might be worse. No Englishmen were fighting in Russia; and anyway Russian deserters would not feel kindly toward a nation in whose quarrel they had been forced to fight. Stumbling over the doorstep into that choking atmosphere, where a few incurious loungers awaited us, I remembered, or was providentially reminded of, a poor devil I'd met once in Leicester Square – a mute. As well as pity, I'd felt a kind of frightened awe. And instantly, while the faces of the lounging soldiers, yellow in firelight, were still new to my gaze, while I still stumbled on the threshold, I determined to borrow that unfortunate's affliction and try whether it might save me.

The rest of the company surged in after me, and one fellow, who seemed more sober than the rest and to have some kind of authority among them (a risky position among deserters, I should think), addressed me, while his comrades sprawled beside the fire or stood swaying in groups, their arms about each other's shoulders. I don't know how long they'd been there, but the place was already reduced to that squalor which soldiery creates when released from inimical discipline. People talk of the good effect of military discipline. The only lasting effect of it I've seen is this reaction against it.

When he stopped speaking I made my gambit, uttering the grunts and gasps I remembered, that strive painfully and in vain for expression. I think I did them well, for the sound made me shiver as the original of it had – though I may have shivered with cold this time. A man mimicked the sound. The fellow who'd addressed me, scarcely looking round, struck him across the face with the back of his hand. Tears came into the offender's eyes, and an expression of stupid surprise, but he did nothing. A kind of discipline still prevailed there. The leader, whose blow had been struck more in assertion of his authority than in defence of my helplessness, I thought, stood eyeing me. I treated him to a bit more gibberish, wilder this time. I can't say that the wildness was introduced with wholly conscious purpose, but when another soldier, beside me, fell on his knees and seized my hand to kiss it, I knew that, consciously or no, I had been aiming at some such response.

Russia then was peculiarly susceptible to the mystique of holy men. I don't know where the cause lay. Perhaps in the national temperament; perhaps in the failure of established powers and a growing doubt of voices of conventional authority. Whatever the reason, many Russians had come to believe that God would speak to them, if at all, only through the lips of men whose holiness was scarcely to be distinguished from idiocy. And in answer to the demand a tribe of them had appeared, sincere and fraudulent, wandering the land frantic and ragged, each with a greater or lesser band of believers who showered on him their money as abundantly as they did their hopes. One such had commanded the ear of the Tsar. I didn't aim so high. I wanted the veneration of a band of drunken deserters. In the desperate, credulous bewilderment of those days the hope wasn't far-fetched, fantastic though it sounds now. I dare say I was wild enough in appearance for the part, and certainly I was wild enough in spirit to attempt it.

I made a gesture of blessing over my first disciple's head. He bent it lower, to kiss the snow-sodden sacking about my feet. I was aware that the others were silent – more silent than they had been when their leader spoke. They stood, still swaying, peering at me through mists of intoxication and illiteracy to see whether I was the one who would save them. The leader was puzzled, uncertain. If I didn't win him I might lose the lot; and in order to win him I must make the next move. Disengaging my ankles from the grasp of my convert, I strode past the leader – brushing him aside and he offering no more resistance than the man he'd hit – to a table strewn with loaves and bottles, all stolen probably. The table was in the same improvident mess as everything else – bottles overturned, wine and spirits drooling onto the floor or soaking into half-eaten chunks of bread, candle wax falling on other bread, candle flame charring other. I seized a bottle and set it to my lips, not without a shudder of repugnance. Not too much, now, I told myself. Only a sip, no matter how frozen you are. It's heady stuff, you're starved, and if you don't stay sober you won't stay alive. Besides, it was done chiefly to signify my assumption of power. Over the tilted bottle I surveyed the crowd. They watched me expectant, docile. The leader too was won, I reckoned. I who had pushed him aside and taken wine without leave must have the right to do so. I took a piece of loaf from the table with my other hand and stood munching it, to allay the pains of my empty stomach and to offset the sway of the spirits. The wood which blazed in and all about the stove threw a fierce heat on my back and legs, but the pleasant pain couldn't be too hot for me.

The man who had mocked was crawling toward me on all fours, penitent. He tried to repeat his comrade's act of devotion. I wondered what was the right response in a holy man. Better not let them suppose I was all love and gentleness; I might have need to terrify them before the night was much older. I spurned the supplicant with my foot and he fell back among his comrades' legs. I think that act of wrath won them completely. Except a few too drunk to bother, they all came forward for my blessing. There I stood, distributing salvation and damnation, and trying not to laugh in the insane excitement of my deceit. I blessed the leader with special fervour, and resting my hand on his head (I had cause afterwards to suspect it had been lousy) I felt I grasped a solid assurance of escape. I insisted on his drinking, often and deeply. There wasn't room for two sober men in this party. A man offered me a religious medal, on a chain, from about his neck. Another pressed a handful of coins on me. I reckoned the holy men had a lively system of tithes going – on best biblical warrant, of course. I accepted the gifts, because I must set a precedent for taking other offerings in a minute, even before they were offered. I had my eye on a handsome revolver in a holster, complete with a belt of cartridges, which one man was wearing. Stolen from a corpse, of an officer, probably. I'd already put a bottle of colourless spirits and a nearly whole loaf in the pockets of my coat.

Having blessed the lot of them, I advanced among them, grunting and moaning as if in a frenzy of inspiration. Taking the ugly head of my chosen disciple gently between my hands I made a show of kissing it on both cheeks, and while he was still reeling under this special grace I unbuckled the revolver belt with equal gentleness. I wasn't unaware, even in the full tide of success, that there was great risk of this appropriation betraying me, or at least incurring the owner's revenge, but my position if I failed now would be no worse than if I didn't try. The revolver was a model unfamiliar to me. I aimed at the ceiling and pulled the trigger. A satisfactory detonation answered, and the congregation, including the victim of my theft, shouted approval. I laughed ferociously. It wasn't all acting. I was a little mad that night. Holding the revolver and making signs of benediction with it I backed to the door, still grunting and moaning. The deserters followed me, some on their knees, exhibiting such a lust for subjection that I thought they deserved what they were getting. On the platform of that wayside station I held a kind of service or audience, waving the revolver in the sign of the cross at the soldiers, who chanted and laughed and wept in response to my unintelligible enunciations. Still gibbering and gesticulating, and still facing them, I dropped from the platform onto the line and strode to where the horses were tethered, my own with them.

But I didn't untie him. I must have a swift horse now. It felt like betrayal, basest ingratitude. I don't think he shared this sentimental view. I hope they looked after him well. He deserved it. Patting him in farewell, I untied one of the cavalry mounts and clambered awkwardly into the saddle, hindered by bottle and loaf and gun and cartridge belt.

My brief disciples were still on the platform, watching the apotheosis of their saint. All except the leader. He hadn't drunk quite enough, and a glimmering of the truth impelled him toward me. With great pleasure, and an accuracy commendable in the circumstances, I shot him in the leg, and as he fell I urged my new mount to a gallop and was borne into the darkness much faster than I had expected, a howl following me which might have been one of rage or continued adoration.

III

I was doing pretty well for one comparatively unused to horses and firearms. But I was used to life, you see, and a wish to stick to that familiar state develops all kinds of skills in a man. You may think I would have done better to get a night's rest and shelter at the wayside halt and resume my journey at daybreak. But I didn't know that I could have kept up my deception that long, and they weren't company I would have trusted five minutes with my eyes shut. Besides, deserters might have their own fate hanging over them, which I'd no wish to share. No, I was better out here, wrapped in the blanket of the dark. A blanket embroidered with stars now, their light striking an eerie sheen from the snow. The darkness was friendly, companionable even, shutting from my notice the infinite emptiness of the land and nearly letting me suppose myself in England, riding home to friends and dinner. But such fancies were as dangerous to me as mirages to the desert-traveller. I must keep a clear head. I must count and re-count the facts, while the hoofs beneath me beat a rapid rhythm and sent scuts of snow flying.

The effect of the spirits I'd drunk didn't last long against the cold. I remembered covetously the sheepskin coats I'd seen on some of the soldiers. I hadn't dared push my extortions that far. But I had food and drink, a faster horse, a weapon. My only remaining needs – short of a clear road to Archangel – were shelter and sleep. The need of sleep was imperative. I'd had none in forty-eight hours; and the last before that had been fitful, broken, apart from their systematic waking of me at short intervals, by the pain suffered in my latest 'conversation' with Captain S and by planning the escape. I must sleep again soon. Where could I sleep? In all white Russia, that reminded me of a great bed spread with linen, there must be some spot for me to lay my head.

My new horse was no friend. He would serve if he must and master if he could. That's a fine game when you're fit; but I wasn't equal to it, and a weary contest we had, though always keeping our speed and the tattoo of hoofs. To make it worse, the stirrups were fixed uncomfortably short, and I couldn't for the life of me find how to adjust them, so in the end I rode without, as I had on my previous mount. That had been all right on the plodder. It was a different thing now, when I had a tendency to nod nearly asleep and loosen the grip of my legs. But somehow I stayed on and we went on.

The fire in the waiting-room was only a distant point of light, smaller and dimmer than the stars – encouraging proof of our speed. I grinned to think of the mingled emotions I'd left round that fire. I'd been right in guessing that another strike had paralysed the railway; deserters wouldn't have ventured where they might be seen by a passing troop-train. Not even for warmth. Not even on this night of murderous cold when every creature had fled to shelter except me and my horse.

Well, I found no walls to house me that night, but I found wood enough to make the walls and floors and roofs of a whole city of houses, for I found a great forest. And, that affording a wind-break, and even a roof of a kind, though the stars showed through it, there I rested, eating most of the bread and drinking a little of the spirits. For all I could see of it, I might share my lodging with wolves and Cossacks, but rest I must; and now I carried many deaths in my belt of shining cartridges. They were rifle ammunition, but fitted the revolver. I had counted them, and marked each for an unknown foe. I lay with my back against a tree, the horse standing tethered in front of me, so that I was shielded behind and before. I'd found a roll of waterproof strapped to the saddle, and I lay on that, though I couldn't get much wetter than I was already. There were noises all round, as of stealthy approach, but I understood in time that they were made by weights of snow, grown too great for the branches to bear, slithering to the ground. I dared not hold my revolver, for fear of firing it in the stress of dream (and so at best advertising my presence and at worst disabling myself – an accident which would have been no less tragic for being ludicrous). But I put it ready to hand, and fell asleep, trusting the horse to be sentry.

Waking at first light, I found myself cramped and aching but not so cold as I had expected – bar my face, the only uncovered part of me, which was painfully blistered and cracked. I felt a nausea, either from hunger or drink, and ate some bread in an attempt to cure it. The remainder of bread I gave to the horse. Strangely, the world looked grimmer to me that morning, when I'd won so much, than it had the previous when I'd lain helpless within a stone's-throw of a hundred enemies. I suppose my physical stamina, never great and much reduced by my treatment at the fortress, was running down fast, beyond the reach of mental stimulus. The snow-laden trees, showing fragments of grey sky between them, were a dreary picture to me, made worse by their resembling Christmas trees. I think only the mechanical impetus of having got so far put me in the saddle that morning. Certainly no hope did. I might have lain against that tree for ever, for all I looked with any pleasure or interest to the idea of being elsewhere. But I mounted, and went on.

The forest which had served me when I slept only hindered me now I wished to travel. Great twisted roots lay hidden under the snow, waiting to grip and twist a hoof. Miraculously, with a wary disdain, the horse avoided or negotiated them. In places the branches grew so low or the trees so close that I must dismount and lead him. And all the time quantities of snow, dislodged by our movement or by their own weight, were falling on us. I would have re-traced my path and skirted the forest, but the sun told me I was still on a true northward line, and to waste precious energy seemed foolish. As well as obstructing our advance the trees obstructed my view. I might be spied on from near ambush without knowing it. So much fine timber was not likely to stand overlooked. Men would have turned it to their use or revenue in some way and built their dwellings near.

And so it proved. On coming into the open air again at last, I found myself on the outskirts of a village. I was annoyed but not much afraid. I was swift now and deadly. Smoke was rising from a few houses where breakfast was being prepared. No living thing about except a few hungry-looking dogs. All able men, and many less than able, had been conscripted, leaving the rest of their little communities to manage as they could. One of the dogs began to yelp. I couldn't blame him – I would have yelped if my ribs stuck out like that – but it was a nuisance, for it brought the people out. Women, children and old men, as I had expected. Seeing a man on horseback, they gathered in a half-circle and stood watching me, waiting. Their attitudes were neither hostile nor friendly. The hunger which made the dogs yelp made the people silent. They just stood, apathetic. Maybe they thought me survivor of a battle, bearing news of yet another retreat – or a government messenger, maybe, come to announce yet another restriction or requisition. Whatever they thought, it stirred no expression in their faces. There were women among them, some young, and I'd seen no woman for many weeks, yet nothing kindled in me. A lifeless bunch the war had made of us. Even the dog was silent now. My horse alone was in command of the situation and stood aloof from everybody, me most of all, in the consciousness of his superiority. He was well-fed still, because his work was important, so his responses were all right. In sheer malice of scorn he kicked one of the dogs, which had come too close. I gave him a sharp lash with the whip I'd found among his accoutrements, to mend his manners. The crowd watched impassively.

There was a church in the village – indeed it was the best building there – and now its priest approached from it at a dignified pace. It struck me that the people had appeared not at the barking of the dog but because they were coming from an early service of intercession. All the services in Russia then were services of intercession. I may wrong him, but I thought the priest had the same deportment as my horse, of feeling himself raised above the rest of us because of a full belly. In fact he may have shared every deprivation his parishioners suffered, but he didn't look as if he did. In addition he had a sleek, sly look I didn't care for. I would leave him and the horse to talk to each other; probably they had a common language. But the old josser, all black robe and beard and upside-down hat and silver cross (that hadn't been melted down for the war effort), addressed himself to me. In German. He was setting traps for me. I stared at him blankly. He tried Russian next, and then a mangled Latin. Either he spoke no English or that possibility didn't occur to him. And all the time, as he stood there with his onion-topped church behind him and his minatory God behind that, his eyes were jumping from point to point of my clothes and equipment. They rested more than once on the revolver. I made sure he saw that. It would cool any of his more hot-headed ideas.

When he'd done speaking and we'd both done staring, there was nothing left to do. These people could not help me – I knew I was on the right road, and I should have thought shame to take anything from them – and they would not hinder me. I made my way through them, brushing the priest in hopes that my horse might kick him. But those two understood each other.

Beyond the village the country stretched empty again. I reckoned the priest would report my passing to somebody, perhaps to the General as the nearest military authority; but the system of communications was largely broken down, and I had put enough distance between myself and the fortress – and would put more before news could reach it – not to be worried. Obviously the village hadn't been warned of my escape. The Cossacks were seeking me in the direction I'd last been seen to take. The countryside that way would have been alerted and this way left quiet. Theoretically, motor transport could be enlisted against me when the priest gave the alarm – though I didn't think they'd much to spare; and anyway I doubted its getting far, unless roads I didn't know of had been cleared. Theoretically, too, news could be telegraphed ahead of me faster than I could ride. Theoretically, better riders who knew the country could outdistance and outflank me. But practically, I reckoned the odds had increased in my favour. Only in the matter of escaping from the General's Cossacks. Of the innumerable new dangers I might be rushing on it was useless to speculate. Any one of a hundred accidents or strategies might trip me yet. So far I'd been lucky – and a little resourceful.

Snow began to fall again. We made good speed. The village diminished quickly and vanished, but I could still see the forest, which was bigger than I'd supposed. I was glad I hadn't tried to skirt it. The snowfall was different today – heavy, relentless, sullen. I couldn't see any spirals in it. Today it would crush a traveller by sheer weight rather than art. Perhaps snow has moods and aspects, like the sea, signs to be read by those familiar with it. There was a difference in the fallen snow, too. The sheen of it in the distance was not like yesterday's; but I couldn't define the change, and while I strained my eyes the flakes fell more thickly, hiding the distance. I laughed to see the new snow. It was covering our tracks, which otherwise would have told a plain tale to any pursuer, for I seemed to have the whole white continent to print my horse's hoofs on in whatever dance I pleased, other people not venturing far from their hearths. Visibility shortened and lengthened, according to the volume of snow-fall, but at its longest it never disclosed to me any other traveller, nor any human habitation. Only the snow, still subtly different at a distance with a difference still not to be defined.

Toward nightfall the sky grew red in angry patches. I could recall seeing it no colour but blue or steel in all the time I'd been in Russia, and I wondered what this novelty might portend. 'Shepherd's delight'? I couldn't imagine any shepherd finding delight here. Suddenly, in the failing light, I saw what drove fancies from my head and made me rein in on the spot. I saw what had given the terrain its different aspect. A little way ahead was a wide river.

It stretched out of sight to east and west, nowhere nar-rower than at this point and nowhere bridged, and the whole surface of it frozen. The surface lying somewhat below the level of its banks and so sheltered from wind, per-haps the air there was sufficiently warmer to thaw snow, though not ice, for the snow had not lain thickly and the ice was largely exposed. How deep was it? The river was fear-somely wide, and I was not eager to attempt a crossing with-out knowing what was under me. Congratulating myself on outwitting men, I had forgotten that the terrain itself might set worse traps for me. There seemed a special cruelty in my seeing this obstacle by the last of daylight, as if a child were shown a horror and then its candle were blown out. I looked along the bank both ways. No help there. To avoid the river might mean a long detour; to attempt crossing it might be a short-cut out of all earthly problems. Revolving this diffi-culty, I turned to look the way I had come. And there I saw what made the need of decision urgent. For a mile or so the ground sloped gently downward to the river, and on the sky-line, against a lingering redness, three, four, perhaps more, black shapes were bobbing up and down – horsemen riding toward me at speed. Perhaps the priest had nearer resources than I'd supposed. Perhaps the riders were innocent of any intent toward me. Anyway, I'd better not wait to ask.

I'm afraid of water. All the voyage from England to Archangel I'd had visions of drowning, with the buoy bells tolling for me. Had I survived those terrors of anticipation only to be drowned in a Russian river? I could picture a deep strong current waiting for its prey beneath insubstantial ice. Well, then, I must ride along the bank.

I urged my horse on with every means I knew. I wished for spurs. I used the whip so that it rang out like a shot or the cracking of ice. He was a perverse creature. I think he liked being hurt. I suppose it gave him the fight he wanted. And probably he hoped to throw me. We hurtled through the dark, froth flying from his mouth. Any obstacle we'd met would have been our gravestone, but we met none. All things tangible seemed to give way before us, even the ground seemed left below, and we to leap through air as if that horse had wings to match his frothing mouth and wild starting eyes and streaming mane. I used the whip more than necessary, as if to punish the horse for my cowardice. It was cowardice rather than caution which had bid me avoid the river – an image of peril rather than a calculation of risk. Had I managed the crossing – and this was a late hour in my adventure to baulk at risks – pursuers might have hesitated, and so I should have won an advantage. As it was, I was committed to a straight race, where any superiority of speed I had was probably balanced by their knowing the country. Angered by my folly, I used the whip mercilessly – and was ashamed later to see I'd drawn blood – but I think he scarcely noticed it in his ecstasy. I'd no notion where the horsemen were – my consciousness was narrowed to violent movement and breathless sensation – until a bullet sang past my head. Whoever they were, they didn't know who I was. The General wanted me alive. I knew Russians went in for shooting from the saddle. I didn't fancy my chance at it, still less when shooting behind me from a furious horse, but I turned and fired once, just to let them know I could play that tune too. One of them shouted. I couldn't judge whether I'd hit him or he was warning the others. Now I fancied I could hear the hoofbeats of the pursuit. If so, the distance between us had lessened. Which meant I'd not even an advantage of speed. Outnumbered and outpaced, in strange country, I was near defeat. I'd still the option of trying to cross the ice, but I still shuddered at it. The shooting had driven my horse to even greater speed: the ground beneath us, and the frozen river on our left, now scarcely visible in the gloom, streamed away like his mane and foaming saliva. Should I stand and fight? In the surprise of it their impetus might bring them on me unaware so I could pick them off. But if even one lagged behind – and I didn't know how many there were – he might come on me from a blind quarter. And their rifles had a longer range than my revolver. But I must chance it. Suddenly I saw a dark obstruction on the river ahead. A bridge. I would make a stand there. Its low parapet would give me some measure of protection. I kicked my feet free of the stirrups, so as to lose not a moment in taking cover when we reached the bridge. But in the excitement of making this plan I failed to convey it sufficiently to the horse; or perhaps he saw his chance of revenge. He made straight on past the bridge, and in a belated attempt to turn him I was thrown. The snow cushioned my fall, but I was stunned, sick and dizzy. One ankle hurt abominably. I crawled to the shelter of the bridge.

That accident was the saving of me. The men behind were guided by the sound of my horse's gallop, for visibility was nil now. They pounded past me in the dark, in hot pursuit of the runaway. Lightened of my weight, he would give them a good run, I reckoned. But I'd nothing else to laugh at. I was lying in the middle of nowhere with a twisted ankle and having lost my horse. The bridge indicated nearby habitations, but that might be good or bad. Practised horse-thief though I was, I couldn't hope for a third stroke of luck. Steadying myself with a hand on the parapet, I hobbled across the bridge, wincing at each step. I could see far lights, twinkling either because of distance or because of trees in front. If I could find a tree I might tear a branch from it for a staff to walk with; assuredly I shouldn't walk far without. My attention was caught by sounds in the dark away on my right. The riders were returning. They must have seen me on the bridge, silhouetted against the lights. A bad blunder. I knelt in the cover of the low wall and rested my revolver – a fiendishly heavy thing it was – on the parapet. The hoofbeats were slower, more resonant now, and not so regular. The leader had ridden onto the ice. I reproached myself bitterly that I was likely to be beaten by a man braver than I. The noise stopped. I removed the spent cartridge from my gun and inserted a new one. They should pay high for their success. The silence endured. Were they stealing toward me on foot? I peered round the end of the wall, trying to see, but although the first stars shone the surface of the frozen river was shadowed by its banks. At whatever risk, I must see what was happening, or I might be surrounded. I lowered myself painfully down the bank and crawled a little way on the ice. A sudden sharp noise of other horses and a shouting of men. The rest of the band must have joined their leader, and had spotted me. Then the moon came from behind the clouds, and I saw the true case.

In the middle of the shining river stood a riderless horse. He was beautiful in the moonlight, and how much more than beautiful to me you may suppose. Beyond him, at the far edge of the wide river, struggling up to their shoulders in water, were my pursuers. My horse had led them onto the ice, which had borne the weight of a horse alone but not that of one ridden. Perhaps the others were heavier anyway. They were fighting to get their heads above water, not helping their masters much in the process. I held out a hand to my horse – the whip hand, I remembered – and called him. He didn't come. But he didn't budge as I crawled toward him, and he let me lead him to the bank and mount there, and in doing this I nearly forgot my fear of drowning. Perhaps he had waited that I might respect myself again and that he might respect me. A foolish thought, but I counted myself entitled to a little foolishness as I turned him north again under the slender moon. Probably he had not returned to seek me; probably he had come by chance, or drawn by some scent from the nearby settlement. But however that was, thereafter we respected each other. There was no more use, nor need, of the whip, and though we were not friends we were a working partnership.

I didn't loiter in congratulation. The floundering horsemen would soon be ashore again. If I'd been practical I would have shot them while they still struggled. But I was never a practical man. We were beginning to pay for our escapades. The horse was tired by his frenzy – perhaps temper more than condition had sustained him till now, for the deserters weren't likely to have looked after him better than they'd looked after themselves – and my pursuers, like drowned men come to life again, were gaining on us as we approached the place where the lights shone. It seemed to be another village, bigger than the last, and was likely to be the end of my jaunt, I reckoned. My horse's hoofs struck a cobbled street. The cobbles had been lately cleared of ice, and sparks flew out. I rode under an arch, on what appeared to be a continuation of the street, only to find myself in an enclosed yard. No time to mend my mistake. I pushed the heavy wooden gates of the archway shut and forced the bolts home.

Two walls of the yard were blank, one contained the gateway and the fourth was the front of a house. A handsome and substantial house, where lights glowed from many windows. I limped up the steps to the door and rang its bell. A long pause ensued. I heard my pursuers come clattering into the village, ride a little way past the gate and stop, baffled. I dared not ring the bell again, for it had seemed to peal out

41

widely in the frosty air. I had turned, gripping my revolver and tensing myself for their onslaught on the gate, when the door behind me was opened. An old man stood there, taller than I, who am tall, and broader. Long white hair, ambiguous dress that might be master's or man's, one hand holding high a lamp which lit and shadowed his face strangely, the other holding wide the door. He noticed my wild appearance and my gun, and, nothing daunted, backed into the hall, beckoning me to follow, with a gesture at once authoritative and courteous. When I stood inside and had secured the door myself I looked at him again. Patriarchal was the word that came to mind, prompted perhaps by several dim old paintings on the walls behind him, in which Biblical figures, not unlike his, were depicted in the same chiaroscuro that the lamp gave him. Somehow he invited trust. I said, 'I am English.' He shook his head and replied incomprehensibly in a deep-toned voice like a bell. Obviously he had assessed my exhaustion at a glance, for I found myself conducted upstairs to a bedroom where a fire was quickly kindled, where a hip-bath was filled with steaming water by a woman who might have been his wife or servant, where a night-shirt of coarse linen, too big for me, was laid ready and where wine and hot food were brought to my bedside. During these proceedings, all managed by the woman, I heard loud talk below of several voices, my host's voice tolling over them, and then the voices stopped and a noise of hoofbeats diminished into the night. Having eaten and drunk, I was left alone, clean and warm again – which I'd thought never to be – and relieved of all responsibility like a child. Who the old man was, why he'd taken me in and shut my hunters out, I didn't know and didn't for the time require to. This dream of safety and warmth was not less real than the long dream of the snow. I fell asleep.

IV

Once I rose in the night, feverish I think, to see where my horse was stabled, but I couldn't find the place and went back to bed and slept again until woken by the woman bringing me hot chocolate to drink and white bread and butter.

I meant to leap from bed immediately I'd breakfasted and resume my journey, but languor held me there, and apparently I was not expected to rise, for the fire was made up and I was left alone to watch the icicles which hung outside the window. They dripped and dwindled a little while, in a brief gleam of sunlight, but soon re-formed and hardened. Soon after that, or so it seemed, but I think I had slept, the room began to darken; and then I did put off the blankets reluctantly and sitting on the edge of the bed begin to dress myself. My clothes had been dried. My broken shoes had been replaced by a pair of riding-boots – not new but sturdy. A hat of sheepskin, with earflaps, had been added to my wardrobe. And tucked into one of my mittens were several bank-notes. I wept a little at these kindnesses. The respite, while mending my weakness had also made me admit it, and so I wept a little. The flesh seemed to hang limp from my bones, and the bones to ache. Before I'd done dressing, night was come, and I'd only the firelight to finish by. I hobbled downstairs. My ankle was no better, but the boot gave it some support.

I found the old man reading a little book – ridiculously little it looked for his great frame – and drinking tea. I tried to signify with gestures my gratitude for his gifts and my intention of departing. I suppose the latter was evident, and the thanks he seemed to acknowledge and dismiss. He filled a glass with tea for me. His hands were big and capable but trembled a fraction. A pathetic tremor it seemed to me, an evidence of vulnerability – of wounds already received, perhaps, and not to be healed – in that seemingly invincible old body. He spoke at length while I drank the tea. At first I supposed it ordinary speech, but soon a chanted quality in it persuaded me that he was praying for me, and that the little book he held, and appeared to consult, had been taken up with that purpose. When he'd done he rose, grasping my hand – or my arm, rather, in the old Roman manner – and lit me to the door. My horse was waiting, groomed and gleaming, held by a boy. I wished I had something to give my benefactor or some word to say. Instead, from the saddle, I bowed, hand on heart. It was done awkwardly enough, and in any other setting would have felt foolish, but I believe sincerity lent it grace.

The boy held the gate open for me. Outside I turned to wave. Already the boy was pushing the gates to again – obviously it was thought wise to keep some posture of defence after the night's alarms – and through the narrowing gap I caught my last glimpse of the old man, holding his lamp lower now, and of the lit windows above his head. Then the gates met, my horse struck sparks from the street again and we were through the village and into open country.

I never knew who the old man was. Attempts to trace him after the war were thwarted by the chaos and worse turmoils which had befallen Russia. I never knew why he had befriended me. I know now no more than I guessed at the time. It was near enough, perhaps. I believe I had reminded him of another fugitive, who had found no help or refuge – a son or grandson killed at the front. Few families in Russia then were spared bereavement. I believe I was helped for the sake of that other traveller, by a wistful gesture which, directed to him, could reach only me. But how much of my case the old man knew or divined is for ever mysterious.

I never knew who my pursuers were, either. Certainly

they weren't Cossacks. Probably men called out by the hostile priest. I saw no more of them. My host had belled them to damnation with the energetic tones of his voice. His manner and his house suggested that he was of some standing in the community. I like to fancy them still searching that snowbound countryside, perpetually re-enacting their misadventures. But they must be old now, if they live, and probably prefer to keep the fireside and tell the tale their own way.

I had received more than physical benefit. I had learned that I might find friends in Russia. Lately it had seemed to consist of snow and enemies. Not enemies in the sense of their feeling a personal animosity toward me – that would have been better – but men who sought to curtail my liberty, and perhaps end my life, as a matter of duty. True, my benefactor's act might have had no more personal feeling than theirs, but at least I knew that not every hand in Russia was raised to hurt me. At the same time I was appalled by the realisation of how much my luck and how little my own wit had done in saving me. It was as if I rode with a fate upon me, preserved for some end other than a wayside capture. Other, but not necessarily better. I must not think that.

Espionage is a bleak climate, causing, perhaps demanding, austerity and arrogance in its inhabitants, and for that reason, I suppose, attracting men with a taste for solitude, with a distrust of others and themselves. But I had been humanised by my recent experience of kindness. I felt held on course by the interest and affection of other people. I wasn't a machine, functioning in isolation. I wasn't even a scarecrow any longer, despite my unkempt beard and hair. I was a man. A man on a horse. A man with a cousin called Gloria who laughed. A man in whom his government felt some interest.

My horse too was revived. But I held him to a canter now. I'd learned that his reserves weren't limitless. Archangel might be distant by a journey of days or weeks. I shouldn't get there sooner by exhausting him. I began to lust for a map, as men in a desert crave water – and with about as much prospect of getting it. It was all very well saying North to Archangel. I might hit a point many hundred miles wide of it. I must have a map. I hadn't thought of looking for one at the house. Surely in a house that had books and pictures there were maps too. I nearly turned back, but the closing gates had seemed to signify that that episode was finished; and besides, I'd made it a superstitious rule never to go back.

I looked back, though. The slender moon was up again. No snow falling – nor had any fallen all day, I think – but what had fallen before lay firm, and figured into strange shapes against a few trees which stood at the approaches to the village. The scene was so sharply defined by the moonlight – the trees, the houses with my benefactor's roof dominating them – that it was etched in my memory for ever. But when at last I got to maps again, I could not find it. Perhaps it was too small to be marked. Perhaps it was razed in the later fighting: a few houses are easily destroyed. Nobody knows anything about it. No map acknowledges it. Yet I've only to shut my eyes to see it again, and feel the cold, and hear a dog that barked at my passing.

Steadily on. The night passed monotonously – so monotonously that I wished for a watch to show me some change in it. You'll end by wishing for too much, I told myself. Be grateful for what you have. I tensed my legs to feel the boots against them and pulled the earflaps of my hat further down.

But oh, I was wistful for that village, for that house. Had I chosen, I believe I could have stayed there for the rest of my life, accepted as a son. And indeed what was I hurrying back to England for? A girl's smile? A sense of duty done? Perhaps. Perhaps just to hear my language spoken by natives again. The loss of verbal communication was worse than I'd expected.

You may think it odd that I'd been given this mission, speaking no Russian. I can only suppose that of the Russian linguists available none had the knack of memorising military plans and orders at a glance. Oh yes, I could reproduce a document written in Russian – as a camera does, understanding no more of its meaning than the camera. It was for this knack, this superior party-trick, that men spoke me fair at the War Office and the Foreign Office. If any of the linguists had the knack, he had also the sense to keep quiet about it. And they were old, scholarly men, I fancy: certainly the translators I met in the course of my work were. Russia hadn't then attracted Western attention as it has lately, and young men saw no good in learning its language. Of course we had diplomatic sources of information, but you can't see everything from an embassy window. So I, who could reproduce in accurate detail what I saw for a few minutes and who didn't mind living rough, was given the job. Not that I'd expected it to be this rough.

Having slept most of the day, I needed no sleep and I determined to regain lost time. Toward dawn there was a change in the terrain. Our path began to drop, and at the same time wooded ground began to rise on each side, making the descent seem steeper than it was. Well, any such change was pleasant after so many level empty miles; and when at sunrise birds called among the trees – you would scarcely term it singing – I felt I was coming into a good country. These trees, like those others where I'd camped, were shaggy with snow, but I liked the look of these. Daylight showed me that the forest extended farther ahead than I could see, keeping the same height above the track. It was a track, I supposed. But my recuperation in the village had made me sanguine, and I looked to meet friends as well as enemies. A couple of days ago I should not have liked my position relative to the trees, for the bases of them were about level with my head and offered a good place of ambush. But this morning I went forward gaily, though keeping an eye on the forest of course. Anyway, I could give a good account of myself. And my nonchalance was justified. At least, it wasn't punished; and that's what practical people mean by justification, I believe. I met nobody. In an hour or two the track widened, the forest sloped to meet it and ceased, and I stood upon the edge of another plain, but this one distinguished by the presence in the middle of it of a town. A prosperous town, walled, with more than one church.

Now a town was as much a novelty in my ride as birdsong, but my response to it was necessarily ambivalent. A town was another matter from a village. There would be officials, a garrison even, contact with other garrisons. No, a town was not for me. I must make my way well clear of it. But there would be maps too. I stood shading my eyes to study the town. Shading them not from the sun but from the glare of the snow. No sign of anybody stirring outside and the walls hid any activity within. The smoke of many chimneys rose in the still air. I pictured wistfully the amenities and comforts of a town. I pictured breakfast served in a warm restaurant, one of those restaurants where regular customers, mostly old, sit for hours playing chess, or reading the newspaper as if a nation's fate depended on their opinion. I pictured barbers who would cut my hair and shave my beard amid the luxuries of hot water, hot towels, steaming copper urns, a scent of pomade and soap. But I was only tantalising myself. Even if news of my escape had not been received here, a foreigner speaking no Russian would be reported to the police, detained and interrogated. And of course the British Embassy in Petrograd knew nothing of me. Official cognisance was innocent of my existence and would continue in that state.

So looking sadly toward the good things I turned away from them and rode eastward, hugging the boundary of the

48

forest and ready to disappear into it at any sign of interest or approach from the town. But the hour was early, the air keen, and the townspeople's business, whatever it was, let them stay within their walls. However, the surrounding country might be watched through glasses: that vigilance would be elementary common-sense in wartime. So I rode on the very edge of the forest, where I might hardly be distinguished from the trees. In the east the plain was bounded by more forest, and I must reach that before I could safely resume my northward route, for on the plain I would be like a fly on a window waiting to be swatted.

But as the day passed the danger of my being seen diminished, and so did my chance of getting much farther, for the snow began falling more thickly than I'd yet seen it, and was blown into great drifts. No room among its close flakes for spirals to form. The air seemed as solidly white as the ground. The town had vanished. My horse suddenly had white gaiters. We were getting deeper into drifts. There was nothing to do but take shelter among the trees and wait.

We waited a long time, the storm not abating. Daylight had nearly gone – more because of the weather than the hour, I thought – when I heard a noise in the forest behind me. A noise of wheels and horses heavy laden and of men's voices raised in encouragement or rebuke. Horse artillery, probably. The forest must be traversed by more than one track. I eased us softly between the trees, as well as the snow permitted, away from the approaching noise but not too far for a view of its cause.

My guess was wrong. The horses that came in sight, a team of four, were drawing not guns but a succession of low wheeled trucks, linked together and bearing chained to them the burden of one great felled tree. Men on foot led the horses; a small boy sat triumphant astride the load, getting clouts of snow in his face from overhanging branches and laughing at them; and the unwieldy conveyance was attended by outriders and people on foot, men, women and children. At first I took this escort to be all foresters and their families, but a little more study showed me that they were wayfarers of several kinds – gypsies, country folk come to market, one soldier with his rifle across his back, mounted on a sorry hack – who had joined the woodcutters for company and for the safety of numbers in these uncertain times.

My interest drew me forward incautiously, and the soldier, who had his eyes more open than the rest, caught sight of me and beckoned cheerfully. At this embodiment of temptation I surrendered. There was only one armed man in the party, I told myself, and my horse could leave any of these far behind. Money for a map was burning a hole in my pocket, as they say; and curiosity was burning a hole in my head, you might add. It would be amusing to put my preserving fate to another test. Most of all, the town was on the route I'd set myself, and deviation might bring bad luck. I walked my horse forward to join the soldier, who rode at the rear of the little caravan.

He addressed me in a friendly tone. Perhaps he took me for a brother in arms. In that case, he must have thought me a deserter, seeing my clothes, but I dare say he had worries of his own. I made my dumb-man noises, this time in the character of one who'd lost his voice in battle. I made a mime of firing a rifle and of clapping a hand to my throat and to my ears. He shouted the story of my misfortune to his companions ahead, who turned and shook their heads sympathetically. The small boy never turned his head back again for the rest of the ride, and got a great many more clouts of snow now he couldn't see them coming. The soldier put an arm round my shoulders. And so, safe in an unquestioning camaraderie, I rode toward the town behind its supply of firewood.

V

We followed a track which the woodcutters must have made on their outward journey, and there the going was easier than it would have been anywhere else, but even so it was a wearisome business. The town jogged and jolted, stopped and started, toward us, but because of its high walls it disclosed no more of itself. Obviously watch was kept, for the gates were opened before the head of our caravan reached them. Guns were mounted on the ramparts. Mostly obsolete. You may imagine that I hung back a little and held myself ready for flight, for I feared an examination of people entering. But we passed in without question or scrutiny. Everybody there was more interested in the timber than in us. I reckoned their stocks of fuel had run low.

We had stopped immediately inside the gates, in a cobbled space formed by the confluence of many narrow streets – alleys, rather – which I could see shooting off in all directions and shooting off branches, so that the interior of the town must be a maze. We had stopped in this space for the good reason that none of the streets beyond could accommodate the timber waggon. The square itself hardly did, and the tree had to be manoeuvred to lie diagonally across it. That done, a gang of men set to work with great two-handed saws. Obviously this work was going to engage the people, actively or as onlookers, for some time, and I was free to explore. The soldier who had befriended me made the motions of drinking, and I willingly followed him to a grog-shop. It was wise to make my debut in the town with a sponsor.

The shop was thick with tobacco smoke. It was cold – perhaps by design, to increase the demand for spirits, but more likely because of the fuel shortage. The men here, like those I'd seen in the square, seemed chilled and dirtied by the weather. I matched them well on that score. Several were soldiers – but of various regiments, thus allaying my fears of the town's being a garrison. They must be on leave, official or 'French'. The rest of the company might have been anything. Anything but prosperous. They had a look of petty shopkeepers and merchants. My companion treated me and declaimed my story to the room. There was a momentary turning of faces to me, a momentary appearance of gesturing hands from the warmth of cuffs and pockets, a short chorus of fatalistic cries, but my professed plight did no more than ripple the surface of that pool of discomfort and depression. A moment later the company had resumed their first attitudes and the proprietor was washing glasses again. This reception couldn't have suited me more. Henceforth I should be accepted here, taken for granted, not given a second glance.

The soldier and I treated each other in turn. We didn't enlarge the round beyond ourselves and I was glad of that, for I must conserve most of my money for a map, perhaps a watch, lodgings and the further journey. My horse too would incur me expense. I had tied him within sight, for he was better than average and might tempt a thief. I smiled to find myself, who had stolen him, assuming the airs and suffering the anxieties of proprietorship. My companion, with pains, wrote for my benefit some of the gossip that was passing. I indicated I couldn't read. Illiteracy was common enough in the ranks. We ate black bread and some kind of pickled fish with our drinks, but after a while my head began to spin and I took that as a sign I should depart. I clapped my new comrade on the shoulder in farewell. That wasn't enough. We must embrace and rub faces before I was released.

I led my horse through the streets. My ankle made walking difficult, but it was easier than bending myself flat for the many low arches that traversed the way. These arches were designed to support the opposing walls of the houses, which might otherwise have fallen inward, I thought, rather than for any visual effect. There were shops, but I couldn't find one that sold maps. I kept returning on my tracks without knowing and finding myself in the square again, where the work of sawing continued with unremitting vigour in the sawers and unabated interest in the crowd. The streets were muddy, and a sickly-sweet stench of bad sanitation was clamant in them despite the low temperature. But fair flowers grew in that bad air. The girls I passed had a beauty which poor clothes could not hide nor their hard lives yet spoil. One in particular I chanced to pass several times in trying to negotiate the maze of streets, and I began to look for her and smile at her. She didn't smile in return, but her eyes shot at me that level glance which is forceful like a gunshot. I didn't suppose that my personal attractions had won her interest. I didn't underrate them, of course, but they were hidden by dirt and rags and beard. No, in that town my horse and revolver and cartridge belt seemed badges of riches – were themselves riches, indeed. And getting money or goods was as vital a business to each there as the getting of fuel. Prices in the grogshop had indicated either that food was scarce or that the currency was not trusted. Probably both. I had noticed that for tenders of gold coin the prices were lower than for those offering paper. So the owner of a valuable horse and arms might win favouring glances were he a more repulsive sight than I. One must live. Time for discrimination later. At my last encounter with the girl that afternoon she passed through the gate of a house, pausing that I might note the house and glancing back to signify that I needn't think myself shut out for ever.

Well, this interchange of glances was eloquent, and I went away pleased. You may think I'd no business to be following strange women. Harsh phrases like 'dereliction of duty' may be on your tongue. But I had business, and urgent business, in the affair, for you remember I'd found no map in the shops. Therefore I must look for one in a private house, and that might be managed better with a woman's help. But there were obstacles. However desperate, no woman wants a dumb suitor. I'd have done better to steal a guitar – or a balalaika, as they call theirs – than a gun; then at least I could have serenaded her. As it was, I should need every personal charm I could muster. I must have myself barbered and try my luck without words or music to woo with. All for a map, d'you see? – brighter then to me than any eyes.

But the barbers' shops were shut. Presumably their chief trade was shaving, and that was done early in the day. So I must find a night's lodging before I could be made presentable to pursue my romance. Inviting as my lady's glance had been, these matters proceed by ordained and regulated steps even in a starving society. Besides, I was enjoying a sense of my daring. Alas for my self-counsel of clear-headedness! Of course I had walked boldly in Russian towns before; but then Mikhail had been with me, and then I had not been sought by the secret police.

I went round the town looking for my soldier acquaintance, that he should vouch for me at a lodging, but I couldn't find him. Nor did I see anything more of my full-figured, black-eyed charmer. The house into which she'd disappeared was shuttered, and my impression of a watcher within may have been fanciful. The winter day was darkening. Christmas must be close now. Not that I should know a Russian Christmas if I saw one, and anyway this hard-pressed town had scant means of celebrating it. Up and down the greasy streets I went – riding now despite the inconvenience, for my ankle was protesting – until, exhausted, I returned to the grogshop, the one place where I should be received without question.

There were fewer drinkers now, but obviously the tree had been divided, for the stove glowed red and its light – the only light there – soon attracted more customers, my soldier among them, by the look of him newly risen from sleep in some frowsy hiding-hole. He remembered me, exuberantly, and we had more embracing and kissing as if we had been apart for months. But he was a good-hearted fellow. I hope he lived.

As afternoon wore into evening and evening into night it became apparent that I need look no further for a lodging. It was obvious that many of the customers intended spending the night here – some were already asleep indeed – and that the proprietor had no objection. It was good for trade, I suppose, and probably, like me, they had nowhere else to go. Russia was full of drifters who had long lost sight, perhaps even remembrance, of any place they'd ever called their own – who had abandoned the hope, and perhaps forfeited the right, of ever returning to it. But none of them could be exile from a farther place than I, I thought with melancholy pride as I settled myself to sleep. I could sleep securely here. It was a different kind of company from the deserters'; and my new friend, in an excess of brotherly love and intoxication, had laid himself to rest across my legs. It wasn't a comfortable arrangement, but it protected me from approach, my head being to the wall, and gave me a watchdog too. I hoped my horse was as safe. I must rely on him to give the alarm at any attempted theft.

It was a funny place to sleep in. And when I woke from dreams, as I did often, to see the foreign faces in the light of the stove and the figures blanketed in coats, the reality was stranger than the dreams.

When I awoke properly daylight was seeping in at cracks round the shutters and the proprietor was extinguishing the stove by pouring a bucket of water into it. This may have been the best method, but I suspected he chose it because it added to the general discomfort and inconvenience of things. The water flooded the wooden floor, bearing ash and charred flakes of log, and formed puddles and rivulets on its way to wet the nearest sleepers. I drew my cramped legs from under the soldier and stumbled between inert bodies to the door. My horse was still there. The air was free of snow and very cold.

The barbers' were shut. I dared wait no longer, lest another stranger come riding into town better mounted and with two guns at his belt. Lurking at the girl's gate in the winter dawn I must have looked more like a murderer than a suitor, and indeed I felt more inclined for that work. I cursed her as an obstacle in my way rather than blessing her as a means of advance, and I was more eager to learn the breakfast arrangements of the house than the charms of its inmate. I opened the gate softly and stole into the garden beside the house. Nobody was about. A bird was singing in a cage on the house wall. Singing to break your heart, and his too. God knows how he had survived the night. I wanted to release the poor little beggar, but it wouldn't be a good beginning. Besides, he was fed here, presumably, and in the open air wild birds might attack him. I knew well the problems of the escaped prisoner. The garden, white and crystalline, might have seemed a romantic place to somebody in another state of mind. The house had evidences of grandeur – a crumbled coat of arms over the door, an elaborate flight of stone steps – but the grandeur had gone before this generation, I reckoned, and even before the last. I looked at my footmarks, shallow in the frozen snow; I looked at the caged bird; I looked through the bars of the iron gate at my horse in the street, as if one of us also were caged. And I wondered what I was doing. There was no useful answer: I could only go on doing it. Despite the girl's encouraging glances, the house looked inhospitable. She might be knotted in by father and mother and relatives and chaperones, dragons innumerable. She might be practising her first wiles on me, with no wish to go further. At best, she might expect an elaborate verbal courtship. And then I smelt coffee, and my doubts died under its benevolent influence. At the same moment a man of indeterminate age and occupation came out of the house, stared at me without surprise, much as I had stared at the singing bird, and went in again. A few minutes later I heard shutters thrown back above my head, and looking up I saw my nymph leaning out in a state of undress which should have warmed my blood even in that freezing morning. But beyond an academic acknowledgment of her attractions I felt nothing except a strong wish that she would invite me indoors. For a long minute she stared at me, gravely, unsurprised, and then drew back more because of the cold than for modesty, I thought. The shutters were pulled to again, I paced the garden walk again, the whole comedy might have ended. But soon she appeared at the door, extinguished now in her dark clothes. I went to her, though she made no invitation. She made no protest, either, but led me into the house.

And there my fears were realised. I was presented at a table where elders and children sat about a coffee urn. My supposed riches were going to spread pretty thin if they had to supply this lot. My eyes went to the urn. Their eyes went to it, too. We were agreed on our priorities. But an old man remembered his manners and addressed me. I did my panto-mime again of having been struck mute and deaf in battle. A white-haired woman rose and came to me and kissed me. I felt pretty low. Obviously I was receiving a kiss that be-longed to some lad of the family who might never tell the story of his wounds – let alone lie about them. I hadn't been badly brought up – I'd been told the right things to do, even if I hadn't seen them done much – and this deception was a grim business. But the alternative was grimmer. I saw that the lie had furthered my suit with the girl, and that only made me feel worse. I didn't even want her, which at that age will squash a lot of scruples. I wanted a map.

I was given coffee first. There was no food. While we drank, bells began to ring in the town. I saw people passing the window. The day must be Sunday. That was why the shops had been shut. The family rose, obviously to go to church, but the girl, with a word of excuse, remained. When the house door banged after them she led me upstairs to that

room from which she had looked down, and there she removed her clothes without pretence of modesty or ardour,
as a thing to be done, a necessary task like drawing water
from the well. The emergence of her white limbs, sturdy yet
shapely, from the rough clothes was like the bursting of a
flower from an unpromising bud. But it was an untimely
flowering, a tender growth that showed itself too soon and
was killed by cold expediency. She unfastened her hair, and
its length fell to her waist. By nature or art her eyes were
bigger and darker than an English girl's. So she stood waiting.

I hadn't expected our bargain to be concluded so abruptly.
The time of day, with its harsh whiteness, was not congenial. The flesh of us both was dimpled with cold. She
turned an ikon to the wall. You can't be ardent about a
necessary task. I was thinking of a map and she was thinking of her people to be fed. Seen in the cold light of reason,
that controlled uncontrol is questionable even when not
used commercially. And the cold light of a Russian dawn is
very like that of reason. And all the time the bird was singing.

When it was done we looked at each other compassion-
ately, as two on whom the world had forced a distasteful
action and who had been brought closer by suffering it together. I was troubled as to how I should give her money.
Following her example, I decided the most direct way was
best, and she took the notes without embarrassment. I made
motions of writing, and when she brought me paper and
pencil I sketched a kind of map and signified my need of
one. She drew me to the empty fireplace and indicated on a
clock on the mantelpiece that I should return at five, when,
presumably, she would have got a map. We made our 'au
revoir' as prettily as we could, but it was not a gay business.

The air was full of church bells and the streets were full
of pious folk and the world was no place for me. I returned
to the grogshop and tried drink and sleep as means to be rid

of my self-disgust. But I couldn't afford much drink now and sleep didn't come easy until the stove was lit in the afternoon. My soldier wasn't there. I suspected that an affair of the heart detained him. Well, probably it was honest, unlike mine. When darkness gathered I raised myself from the fireside reluctantly, for there was a fine blaze then, and returned to the house.

Again the family were at table. They were decent people, but I couldn't judge their place in society. Such definition is always difficult in a foreign country and was specially difficult in the Russia of that time, where nobles dwelt in houses an English farmer wouldn't look at and labourers in ruined palaces. This time wine and hot food were on the table. Probably of my providing, for I understood the elders to be thanking me for it. After the meal, of which I ate more than my share, musical instruments were produced and the women in turn danced or sang those airs of passionate hopelessness peculiar to the eastern lands that have still a foot in the west. In both accomplishments the girl excelled, and I was sorry things could not go another way for us. Under the spell of music and wine I almost persuaded myself they still could; but I should have needed to be a different man, on another errand at another time, and potent though the wine and music were, they couldn't work that transformation.

As the evening wore on the women tired; their place was taken by an old man who recited sing-song an interminable ballad; and the strong coffee was breaking the wine's hold on me. Most of all I was sobered by the realisation that there was no sign of the map. Perhaps she was waiting for a chance to pass it to me privily. I signalled that I must go. She accompanied me from the room and drew me upstairs again. I hoped and dreaded that she might intend a repetition of the morning, but in her room, unchanged bar the lighting of a candle, she only shook her head and stretched her arms wide and made a voluble explanation which was gibberish to me and indicated that I should return at noon next day. I was angry at this default, but a moment's thought told me that maps might not be got easily in wartime and that the girl was honest, so I swallowed my anger and we kissed good-night. And despite my regained sobriety I nearly envied that other man on another errand at another time.

The night passed like the previous one. The soldier pillowed himself on my legs again. Sometimes a sleeper shouted or muttered, the same fierce pessimism audible in those outbursts as in the national songs I'd heard. I understood not a word, of course, but the tones must have struck deeply, for long afterwards and far away I still heard them in my own dreams. They seemed to voice all the inarticulate longing and innate despair of that people.

At dawn the proprietor again doused the fire, and soon afterwards I went to a barber's. I don't know why exactly. My overgrown hair and unaccustomed beard were not comfortable; but I think more than that I was impelled by some hope that in being made presentable I might be made that other man who should teach the girl to dance to his tune. Anyway, there was the barber's – not so grand or glittering as I had imagined it, but open at last and good enough. Several customers were waiting, and I sat at the end of the line. We waited in a row of chairs, each chair facing its own mirror and basin, and the barbers worked their way along the line. The shop was warm and steamy. Newspapers were available, printed in that frightful Cyrillic lettering which I could memorise so easily and never understand. The wall behind us was covered by posters – advertisements, official announcements and such – many of them pictorial, and I amused myself by looking at the pictures in the mirror, for the text was as good to me backwards. And so I had the strange experience of staring at myself once in the mirror and again in a reflected poster. The vanity of youth had made me familiar with my face, but I hadn't expected to see a price over it. I'd not been photographed since my arrest – because they'd not reckoned on my escape, I suppose – and so an English photograph had been used. Luckily I was not recognisable in my ragged, bearded state as that smooth-faced, blazered youth, straw hat under arm, surrounded by the honest fakes of a photographer's studio. I wondered by whose carelessness – to give it no worse name – they'd got the photograph. I knew already that one link of my chain of contacts in Russia was false; now I got a whiff of something wrong at home.

At that moment the barber reached me. I saw his hand ready to shave me – and so reveal me as the man in the poster, and cut my throat as surely as if he did it with the razor outright. I grabbed his descending hand, leapt from the chair with gesticulations that were meant to be explanatory but must have appeared lunatic, and ran from the shop to my horse, followed by the barber in person and by the astonished gaze of all the customers.

VI

I don't know whether I was hotter or colder with fright. I was both in turn, and my heart didn't beat normally again until I'd ridden several miles. Even then my head ached from the scare I'd had.

And so I never knew what my luck would have been with the girl if I had returned in more handsome guise, nor whether I might have mended our bad beginning. Sometimes I imagine I could have won a Russian wife, and still be there, walking in and out as master under the repaired coat-of-arms, sitting in the garden when the snows were melted from it to drink tea, and in winter at the fireside of nights hearing my wife sing those songs which would have reminded us of my first night there. Equally, I shall never know whether she, or others through her, were delaying me on a pretext while inquiries were made. I was torn from hands that might have held me, loving or harmful, and re-claimed by the wilderness.

The empty snows were harder to face after my respite from them; the wind howled like the voices of all who had ever despaired and perished in it. As if the wilderness had marked me for its own and would punish me for my defec-tion. But my horse bounded into this desolation with the pent-up energy of arrow from bow. He embraced it. He laughed to see it. I suppose he was tired of inaction and strangers. We made an ill-assorted pair – he ardent, I balanc-ing the sum of my dealings in the town like a regretful ac-countant. I say balancing, but it was all debit. I had lost time and money: I had gained nothing. (Except, if you like, the knowledge that my escape was advertised – and I could have guessed that. Except also an effectual rebuke to my foolhardiness. The business of a man on the run is only to run. Henceforth I must do just that, with no clever diversions.)

The snow on the plain had melted somewhat or been shifted by wind during my holiday enough to admit our passage. But I believe if it had been up to my neck I should still have advanced, under the impetus of my lesson. Having skirted the walls of the town – there was only one gate – I rode due north, expecting every minute to hear the guns on the ramparts roar news of my escape, and sounds of pursuit. But the town threw a pall of uninterest over my departing figure. One or two people may have been puzzled, and expected for a little while to see me again, but they would soon forget me amid more urgent matters. I did have some sense of broken tryst with the girl, but that was foolishness.

I saw nobody all that day. Our speed soon diminished the town to a smudge in the snow, and then caused it to vanish wholly – as so many other places and people had diminished and vanished, consumed by my imperative need to reach Archangel. Sometimes I thought I too had been consumed by it, reduced to an incarnate necessity. There was nothing to see in the snow, so of course I saw Archangel, building it in the blankness with a few fragmentary recollections of my first arrival there. Archangel was become an unutterably desirable, incalculably splendid toy that a child sees on top of the pile; and he scrambles over everything else to get it, kicking and trampling; and when he has it he probably breaks it, for nothing can exceed the joy of getting. I imagined nothing beyond Archangel. There was a dim picture of grey waters lapping its quay and of familiar faces on a farther shore, but I dismissed it. Archangel was heaven: once I was there all responsibility would be taken from my hands.

I talked to myself a lot that day. It was a habit I must curb, lest it betray me if I ever get into human company again – which seemed unlikely. On our right, at a distance of a mile or two, the forest still marched – solid, impenetrable. It might extend infinitely. The steely sky that rested on it might extend infinitely. Well, I too could go on for ever, I vowed, trying to clench my chattering teeth. A horseman riding perpetually through a landscape infinite and unvaried would appear stationary – and would in effect be so – but I could do it if I must. I accepted the cold as a just punishment, rejoicing in the hardships of the day as so much less than my folly deserved.

I'd no food. For all my gourmandising in the town I'd made no provision for travel, not even replenishing the spirit bottle, which was two-thirds empty. I'd expected to be there longer, of course, with time for such preparations. But a fugitive has no right to expectation. Well, I must hope the fate which had preserved me so far would throw me some food before too long. I still told myself that if I was preserved indeed, it was only for a worse end. I intended to reach Archangel, but the warning was a necessary ballast to my optimism. What I'd eaten in the town would sustain me a good while, I reckoned, being a feast compared with my previous fare. I stopped once or twice to take a sip of spirits against the cold – stopping only to avoid spilling the precious stuff, for it was no day to stand in. I took no more than a sip. I must keep my head clear; I must conserve what I had; and anyway nothing could ward off that cold for long. The shivering was replaced by a momentary flush of warmth as the spirit went down, as if I'd crossed the flight of a shooting star, only to renew its grip next minute. These halts weren't otherwise encouraging. Riding, I had at least a sense of doing something. Stopped, I was reminded of the apparent futility of doing it. There was nothing to see but the mass of snow and the mass of forest, nothing to hear but the chattering of my teeth and the horse's breathing. Only that puff of steam that rose from his nostrils was pitted against a universal iciness; if that pitifully small and fragile puff were interrupted I should die as surely as if my own breathing ceased.

And the wilderness had not yet visited its full anger on us. As darkness encircled us and drew steadily closer, the silence beyond our dwindling pool of vision was broken by a sound I'd heard before. The wilderness had unleashed on us its wolves.

Listening open-mouthed, as if those voices of perdition issued from my own throat, I shivered more than the worst cold had made me shiver. They sounded to be at some distance still, on both sides, running with us and calling to each other. Was it a nightly gathering or had they scent of us? If they hadn't yet, they would have soon. With luck I could laugh at five of them; but, in the moment of my reloading, a sixth might laugh at me. I wondered whether I might baffle them by stopping. But the idea of the stealthy approach of enemies, I motionless, was as unpleasant to me as it had been on the morning with the Cossacks. Better keep moving, even if toward danger. I had the vivid imagination which is cowardice : I could see my body, and the horse's, torn, living, by those ravening mouths. Desperately culling all the little wolf-lore I'd ever heard, I remembered that they dreaded fire. But I had no means of making any. These thoughts, set down sedately here, were punctuated in fact by the nearer howls of death, which gave them a feverish quality I can't convey. I was like a condemned man trying to plan his escape in practical detail while the chaplain is reading a final prayer. Of course, my revolver would make a brief flash, but that was no good. I needed flames, and lasting ones. Could I set fire with that gunflash to the remaining spirit in my bottle? I didn't know how adulterated it was; it tasted pretty fierce. But even that wouldn't last long enough. I needed dry wood to pour it on. Was there anywhere out of doors in Russia a piece of dry wood after the long snow? Deep in the forest perhaps. Could I reach it? That meant riding through one pack of wolves and then – if there was a 'then' – forfeiting any advantage of speed in order to penetrate the forest. They had scent of us now. A more excited, hysterical, slavering note was audible in their cries. To ride for the forest was to risk death, but to remain on my present path was to seek it. We might break their line in the surprise of the moment. We, I said. My horse, I meant. He was the one who must set his legs among them. I thought his spirit would answer to it. If he faltered we were finished. I had no doubt about my chance with five shots against wolves innumerable. I said nothing special to him. He must feel that I was unworried; so far as the howls would let him he must think it just a good gallop. I don't think I said a prayer as I turned his head. I don't think I even recalled any special face. But I knew it was the moment to do such things had I chosen, for I knew I was running nearer death than I had done yet.

We went through them so forcefully – I receiving through the horse's body a sense of the impact with which his hoofs struck some of those evil bodies, and exulting in the hurt he did – that we nearly stunned ourselves against the first trees of the forest. But there could be no pausing. My tactic had momentarily disconcerted the pack, but in an instant they would re-form and be on us from our rear. I rode among the trees as far as I could, torn and buffeted by unseen branches, and when the way grew impassable to a rider I tumbled off and led my horse, groping with my free hand for dry wood. For a long way – a diminishing lifetime – it was all wet. Then I fancied it was only damp. And at last, in a place where the trees stood so close we could hardly squeeze between them, the floor of the forest was soft not with snow but with fallen needles and the wood was nearly dry.

No time to seek better, for the snarling of the wolves, which had moved uncertainly and at a distance until now, was suddenly closer and purposeful. I fired one shot in their direction and was rewarded by a yell of pain. Ejecting the spent cartridge, I took another from my belt, prised the bullet from it, inserted this home-made blank in the empty chamber and turned the cylinder so the blank should be fired next. I kicked fallen branches and tore living ones into a ring about me, sprinkled spirits on the driest and without much confidence fired the blank cartridge at the bit of wood most heavily saturated. It worked like a dream. The spirit leapt into flame and the flame danced both ways to encircle me.

Not a moment too soon. The wolf faces, held back by the fire and howling horribly at it, were near enough to be seen in every detail. Baffled by the flames, they prowled and turned angrily. As yet they confronted me on only one side, but already one or two were slinking round to try another. I poured more spirit on the wood behind me. The bottle was empty. It had been a trick at home to sprinkle sugar on a reluctant fire, and I remembered with what a sinking heart I had seen sometimes that only the sugar had caught light and that when it burned out the coals would be as lifeless as before. But now the wood too had taken fire. I scooped up handfuls of the fallen needles and added them to the blaze. That done, I had done all I could for my defences. I must turn to thinning the enemy ranks. Still they were prowling and turning, slinking round my fiery fortress, those nearest moving sidelong, those behind jostling to get nearer, but always conscious of me, their eyes fixed on me as if in love.

I must have been feverish, for sometimes I saw the trees moving and the wolves still: but whichever moved, I picked off the right ones, as in a nightmare shooting-gallery. I was able to shoot two of the ugly brutes point-blank before the rest withdrew. They retreated only a little, and there resumed their circling, so I gave them the contents of the other chambers and reloaded. I don't know whether wolves can climb trees, but I saw one trying. If they got into the branches above me, that would not be a pretty situation. I gave him two bullets of the new five in honour of his initiative and he fell among his brethren. None of them attempted to copy his exploit: he remained a solitary pioneer. By now the elder and wiser of the pack had judged the game unprofitable. They drew off, most of the others following. A few mutinous youngsters lingered, but the teeth of their leaders and another shot or two from me shifted them also. I was left feeling a pretty fine fellow. Shouting 'Everything must go!', as they do at sales in the big shops, I fired the last bullet after the retreating shapes and turned to praise my horse for his courage. And saw him held by a man, and saw other men who stood watching me.

Well, I didn't mind having witnesses of my cleverness, but I wouldn't have chosen these. They were gypsies, and their expressions told me I had routed one beast of prey only to be caught by another. I began to reload, but one saw what I was at and sent the gun spinning with a blow of his cudgel on my wrist. Another picked up the gun and examined it. The man who'd hit me tore at my cartridge belt. I tried to save it, and was knocked to the ground by several of them. They pulled me to my feet again, but only to unbuckle the belt. That done, they fell to quarrelling over the division of the cartridges. One man, content with sole possession of a lesser prize, snatched my sheepskin hat. On my attempting to recover my goods, the ruffians were unanimous in knocking me down again, and then relapsed into dissension over the spoils. Now they were tearing the belt to pieces, obviously in hope of hidden gold. One wretch had noticed my good boots and was hauling them off, careless of what happened to me in the process. My coat was torn from me over my shoulders and the pockets were ransacked, so I lost the last of my money too.

All this was done under the approving eye of their leader. He was bigger than the rest, a swarthy hirsute man with gold ear-rings. Possibly he was not a gypsy himself, but had encountered them somewhere and made himself their lord. He took no part in the pillage, but looked on with amusement like an indulgent father watching the games of children.

His standing aloof was probably a sign not of disdain but of the knowledge that he would have his pick anyway. His only action was to kick me repeatedly in the ribs, saying again and again a word that sounded like 'Kurdinska' – I'd forgotten that till now – and laughing. He was the only person I heard laugh in Russia, and I have never hated laughter so much. The others did not laugh when he did, but watched him solemnly. Perhaps they wondered when his temper would turn their way.

When he'd tired of kicking me, and the others had stolen everything of any good, leaving me barefoot, bareheaded and in shirtsleeves, and gabbled their rage at finding no gold and their glee at finding my last few bank notes, they tied my wrists and ankles and carried me away with them. They carried also the carcases of the wolves I'd shot, and I reckoned our prospects weren't much different. I say it lightly now, but at the time I was not light-hearted. I was nearest despair then. I did indeed despair. Now I must escape from these marauders merely in order to go on escaping from the secret police, and I hadn't the energy of morale for it. No good trying my holy-man act on this gang, nor my wounded-veteran act. They didn't care what I was. Even if I could escape, I should be without horse, weapon or sustenance, without adequate clothes even. I should soon be crippled by frostbite, and soon afterwards die of exposure. I wondered why they were taking me with them. Perhaps they hoped to get a ransom, or extort from me the secret of gold. Perhaps they simply wanted the pleasure of hurting me more. They had hurt me for the same reason the owner of the drinking-shop had poured water into the stove: not from personal animosity – they didn't know me as a person – but as their acknowledgement of, and contribution to, a cruel world. I was merely a live thing that might by having pain inflicted on it assuage some of their own. Don't think I regarded them with Christian forgiveness. If I could have got hold of my revolver I would cheerfully have sent them to the next world, better or worse. Failing that, I might in my misery have sent myself there. Being powerless to do either, I could only be carried along with the other carcases, and – because observation was instinctual now – observe my captors.

There were seven of them – small men except the chief – each leading a shaggy kind of pony. My horse was a rare prize, and I cursed to think he would be bestridden by the chief when we were clear of the forest. That ruffian had my revolver already. I saw no other firearms among them, but all carried knives – some plain, some of an Eastern fashion beautifully wrought – and cudgels. I wondered whether they were camped nearby or had turned aside from a journey at sight of my fire.

And all the time I raged or wept at my luck. To have survived so many dangers only to end so wretchedly! I told myself that God was punishing me; but though I had committed offences enough, I didn't quite believe it and pictured the long upper lip Mr Prout, that professional churchman, would have pulled, as nearly sceptical as he dared, had I told him. (Had he been alive to be told, but the distinction between life and death seemed academic here.) It's comfortable to believe misfortune a punishment; it leaves room to hope for rewards too; and people do get through life to their own satisfaction by regarding it as a series of bargains, with prices to be paid and payments to be received. But I was never eager to enter into bargains to which no other party was apparent. Yet still I had a superstitious idea that I had been captured by gypsies because I had broken tryst with the girl. It was nonsense, of course. Our acquaintance had been more profitable to her than to me; her conduct had been quite unsentimental; and by failing our next engagement I had merely lost the chance of a map. I was using the incident as a label for other offences, more deserving of punishment and less avowable – and for shame, perhaps, that men of my age were dying in battle while I followed a more devious trade.

Anyway, the gypsies, whether agents of divine retribution or only accidental, had a firm grip of me and carried me along. But for the circumstances, it would have been a pleasant change of transport, for I was stiff and sore from many days in the saddle. So I was carried, face uppermost, the stars blazing coldly down on me. I traced their constellations and remembered the names of some, but could not read the future in them as men have professed to do. We were still in the forest. I couldn't judge our direction. The howls of the wolves had died away into whatever hell those creatures had issued from, and the talk of the gypsies had dwindled in the business of finding a path, and the silence glittered frostily.

In time we came out of the forest, and I was slung over a pony, face down, and saw only the ground beneath its hoofs for the rest of the way. When I was pulled to my feet again – none too soon, the blood pounding in my head – we stood in an encampment where tents of animal skin were pitched and an iron pot hung over a fire sent out delicious rumours of food. As I'd expected, the leader had ridden my horse; and he remained mounted now – perhaps to be farther from his followers, perhaps to be nearer the stars. There were women in the camp, as ill-favoured as their men. Whoever talks to me about the romance of gypsies talks to deaf ears. And of course there were children and babies at the breast and a rabble of dogs. But after a cursory glance at them, and ignoring their prolonged study of me, I concentrated my attention on the stew-pot. Man reconciles many contradictions. I didn't want to live, but I wanted some stew.

I soon learned that for the moment I was to live and lack stew. They flung me into a tent. It stank, but any shelter from the cold was pleasant. I was left alone there, except the spasmodic attentions of dogs, while the gypsies feasted. Drank too, to judge by the noise. I wondered whether they were dismembering the wolves to augment the stew. Pres-

71

ently the leader came to the tent and set a platter of food where I could eat it if I ate like a dog. And I did eat like a dog, without hesitation. He laughed, but more as if we shared a joke than were at opposite ends of it. He didn't kick me this time, or repeat the word, whatever it was – perhaps those were company manners – and after a moment left me alone to my degraded supping. And after that I slept, burrowing as best I could still bound among the malodorous bedding of the tent, grateful for its warmth. I snatched sleep whenever I could in those days. The rest of life was merely an interval between getting food and getting sleep. Sleep did seem a material thing, to be got, and whether the name Archangel was a prayer before it or a dream in it I could hardly say. I was dimly aware later that people came to the tent, but how many and of which sex I didn't know, for they were gone again when I woke at daylight, and at the time I was aware of them only as a disturbance of my sleep, as so many elbows and knees and feet to be repelled or avoided.

The evidence of their having domestic lives, and affections even, made the gypsies only more abhorrent to me. The wolves too had a family life, but ignorance of it enabled me to regard them as creatures purely evil and accept them more readily.

From where I lay I could see nothing of the world outside but a jagged splinter of daylight between the tent flaps, and I'd no intention of budging from my warm place to see more. An icy draught entered by that gap and cut through the stale air to chill my face, persuading me I was better off where I was. I was even warmer than I'd been all night, since the other sleepers in leaving had thrown their blankets over me – in haste, I imagine, not kindness. So I lay, studying that irregular shape of morning which was the only evidence of the world outside. 'The world outside.' How improbable that sounded. Was there actually a world where life continued orderly and gracious? My senses could attest only to fear, cold, hunger, fatigue; and memory was a weak testimony beside theirs. If another world did exist, of food and comfort taken for granted, of time for thought on things beyond one's animal needs, I was in eternal exile from it, and the remembrance only aggravated my present distresses. As a boy, like many boys, I had invented and enacted stories of adventure. Now I experienced adventure; yet I could hardly say which was less real. (And today, at the other end of life, I'm telling such a story again, and still can't easily say which is least real.)

The silence outside the tent was absolute. I began to wonder whether the gypsies had left me, or whether I had been rid of them by some stroke as fortuitous as my capture. No dog barked, no baby cried. After long speculation I struggled to my feet and hopped to the entrance of the tent. Only to meet the steady gaze of a gypsy who squatted directly opposite the tent holding my revolver. He didn't look intelligent, but obviously the mechanism had been explained to him and he'd been told what to do, so I retreated. Presumably the rest of the tribe had gone on a raid or foraging expedition. I tried to get out another way, but the tent was so made and fastened as to prevent it. The gypsies must have gone far, for a long time passed before I heard their return. Women with their brats came to the tent and I was pulled outside.

So far as I could see the gypsies had returned empty-handed, bar some firewood and a small wild animal, a kind of goat. Even the leader was scowling. But his face cleared at sight of me. Was he still pleased by my capture, or was I to figure in some further entertainment? The fire was made up with the new wood and they cooked breakfast. My hands were unbound so I could eat – a mess of meal boiled in water – but the man with the gun still covered me. There was nothing useful to do for the moment but eat the food and get what good from it I could, to be called on later. If my feet had been unbound I would have snatched a knife and tried to hold the leader as shield and hostage between me and the rest; but it would depend on surprise and was hopeless with tied feet. That was lucky, perhaps, for the leader was stronger than I, and in grappling with him I should be the mark for half-a-dozen knives and clubs; and anyway the man with the gun might not be loath to put a bullet in his chief before putting one in me.

You see that caution was shaping my plans again. I wasn't looking for death quite so hard this morning. Sleep and food had made a difference. So I gobbled down the hot mess, as docile as they could wish. When breakfast was done they began to strike camp. Perhaps it had been intended only as an overnight stop, or perhaps the region had proved less fruitful than they'd hoped. To keep moving was the best bet for a small and comparatively unarmed band, unless they could find an impregnable fastness, in a country traversed by other wanderers reckless as themselves and better armed. The tents were folded and strapped on the ponies' backs. Also the trophies of wolf head and pelt. I was aggrieved by this misappropriation. I should have liked to hang those proofs of valour in a panelled room in England somewhere. (You see how hope was rising.) I must be content with the knowledge that probably I'd eaten wolf. But as if divining my wish, the leader directed that my hands be bound again and one of the grisly pelts flung over my back so that the head rested atop my own – rather as you see in pictures of Roman legionaries. It stank abominably. So, no doubt, did I by then, but I was accustomed to that. My wish was granted, but in a way I didn't quite like. It – and the looks of the leader – boded me no good, I thought. Now my feet were loosened. The men being mounted, I was thrust in front of them to walk ahead with the women (who bore burdens not so much smaller than the ponies' as less important). The women were valued below knives and ponies, and the leader had no apparent interest in them. They set up a skirling, keening caterwaul as we tramped, which a lad accompanied haphazard on a small side-drum. A dreadful row it was, and not enlivening. I felt as if I walked among the mourners at a bizarre funeral. And I soon learned that the effect was not accidental.

When we had walked some way in the open the party stopped and the leader rode alongside me. On my horse. I hoped the horse might throw the usurper and save me again, as in legends of loyal beasts, but he was confused by so many changes of ownership and had lapsed into impartiality. The man gestured ahead, and the women parted to make way for me. Was I set free? I knew better – feared worse – than that, and stood my ground. But it was not permitted. The man lashed me with his heavy whip. The only alternative to being lashed senseless on the spot was to go, so I went.

I was barefoot in the snow, remember, and my ankle hadn't mended. I neither ran nor walked nor hobbled exactly, but got along by a gait that was something of each. After about a hundred yards I looked back. The gypsies hadn't moved. Perhaps I was truly set free. After another hundred I looked again. Still they stood. But at my third looking back they began to move after me, the riders first now, the women following. I went on, glancing back more often. They were gaining on me. The dogs kept running forward of the riders and being called and cursed and whipped back. Apparently I wasn't going fast enough, for the leader waved me on, shouting, and presently encouraged me with a bullet in the snow just short of my heels.

It was to be a hunt, a diversion in their monotonous existence, devised by the leader perhaps to indulge his taste for inflicting pain, perhaps to distract his followers' attention from the faults of his regime. I didn't like to help him in either purpose, but still the alternative was death, and I had begun to picture Archangel and England again. So I ran. It was no worse than Hare and Hounds at school – bar the end – but there I had usually contrived to be a hound. They were holding the ponies and the dogs in check. They wanted the fun to last. I wasn't sure how long it would last even granted their restraint, for I was in poor condition. I should drop before dark however patient my hunters. But before then fate might intervene to help me. So I went on, conserving my strength as much as possible.

We were running in the open, but bounded nearly on either hand and bounded far ahead by dark masses of forest. If fate was going to help me, it gave no sign. Not an animal or bird to be seen, let alone any person. I went – ran, walked, faltered, stopped, started again – in solitude, seeing nothing of the gypsies behind me, only hearing the heavy tread of the ponies, the jingle of harness, the savage voices of the men that were no less savage and no more intelligible than the cries of their dogs. Sometimes these sounds were close, sometimes they fell back. When I stopped, the huntsmen waited. I suppose the leader still wanted to make the sport last and saw I could go no faster. He still cracked his whip, but not to touch me, and he shot at me no more. I reckoned the climax would be pretty bloody to justify this long crescendo.

The universe I ran in was one of sensations: the pain of feet and limbs, the pain of coatless chest bruised by the cold, the stench of the wolfskin. Any thoughts that intruded among these sensations were like dreams and didn't add up. I didn't know how long the chase had lasted, I halting more often and longer, but the sun had moved from over one wall of forest to over the other. When it dipped below those tree tops the light not only of this day but of all my days would be snuffed, I reckoned. And still fate made no intervention. Maybe I'd spent my good luck, drawing on it too heavily of late. Certainly I'd escaped perils of which any one might have finished me, but that was cold comfort to die with.

The air was keener still now. The silence seemed unbroken – I suppose because I'd grown deaf to the sounds of flight and pursuit. The low sun burned red, showing everything with a sad fierce clarity. It was like the afternoon of Christmas Day, when you walk after your heavy lunch to sharpen your appetite for tea. And for this or some other reason I believed firmly that it was Christmas Day. By now I was resting more than I ran. They would finish me off soon, the dogs first and then the men, slowly, for I was providing little sport now. Well, one last effort. I fixed my eye on a point where the walls of forest I ran between apparently met the forest that lay ahead. It was only an apparent meeting, I thought, an optical illusion of distance and dusk, and anyway it was a point far beyond my reach. But that's the right kind of point to aim for, I told myself, recalling a bit of school lore from the recent and irretrievable past. I calmed my panting as much as I could. And let me run clear-headed, I prayed. Not praying to any God, for I didn't think any God was participating, but simply shooting the wish into a void. Let me run clear-headed and remember the old jolly Christmasses at home, for I don't expect I'll think very clearly once the dogs and the knives are busy on me. So with a little gasp – of exhaustion, not despair, for I'd been running in a hopeless landscape for some hours then – I began the last sprint, my vision failing faster than the light, my legs trembling, but my thoughts winging still swift and sure to another country and other times.

I was running slowly, yet the walls of forest seemed to close in quickly. Their lines, so long parallel, must converge here. And their meeting with the further forest was not an illusion. That mass, so long the horizon of the day, lay just ahead now and I saw that the open way I ran on, though much narrowed, penetrated it. I could hear the gypsy band closer. They were drawing in for the kill, afraid of losing me among the dusky trees. Well, I should die among trees. I wasn't sure it was just the place I would have chosen, but I could think of many worse. I was into the new forest, into the narrowed track, and immediately fell over a stump of tree and went sprawling and expected to feel my murderers' hands on me. But I was suffered to go on a little. In picking myself up I saw their faces very near, like apparitions in the gloom. They looked tired – more by the long restraint, I supposed, than by the chase. Anticipation and eagerness were there too, but all overstamped by fatigue. Even the leader's laugh was merely mechanical now, a necessary badge of command. I saw their ghastly faces and the foam-flecked lips of the ponies before turning my head and running on. Falling on, rather, for like my luck my strength was overspent. I advanced only a yard or two before tripping on another tree stump and falling again. This time I didn't bother to get up. I heard a horn blown. They were hunting me with all the proper forms. Another horn answered the first. Come on, get on with it, I muttered. Never mind the music.

But a strange paralysis had struck the gypsies. Raising my head I saw that they stood where I had last seen them, as if the two low stumps I'd fallen over were a formidable barrier. Come to think of it, there was a significance in tree stumps, but I couldn't remember it. The gypsies were looking at me reproachfully almost – those who were looking at me – as if I'd taken an unfair advantage. The chief had abandoned even the semblance of laughter and was turning his head from side to side uneasily like one who hears bad news on the wind. Well, death wouldn't be too bad if it came wrapped in delirium like this. A shot cracked the silence, followed by several in rough unison. But none of them hit me. And the gypsies were in flight, even the one who was dragged by a foot in the stirrup.

I fainted. Probably for only a minute, for I had a glimpse of two or three men in a uniform that was not military, carrying guns, who took hold of me. And then I fainted again, longer and deeper.

VII

And regained consciousness – an unexpected and incredible surfacing – to see myself lying on a sofa of crimson velvet. There was a lot of lamplight and firelight, reflected by innumerable lustres and by looking-glasses of every size. The immediate view was filled by a huge person dressed in white. There was also a smaller man, a doctor perhaps, who busied himself alternately with me and with bottles and glasses on a table behind me, but he went away at some time. I supposed afterwards that I must have been speaking English unawares, for the huge person in white addressed me in English; but at the time I sought no explanation, thinking myself either delirious or in heaven. The first thing I understood him to say, in a playfully grieved tone, was 'You are not Russian. You are not a gypsy. Please! Please!' He sounded so comically affronted by this double failure that I felt I ought to pretend I was one or both; but instead I burst out laughing and said 'Is it Christmas?'

He considered the question seriously before replying 'No'. His enduring bafflement over my identity reminded me of those Englishmen who say 'Were you at Oxford? Cambridge?' and at the second negative regard you as not existing; and I laughed again, on his crimson velvet sofa, all the lustres laughing in sympathy.

I learned afterwards that the gypsies had unwittingly driven me on to an estate. The keepers frightened them off and, supposing me to be one of the gang, took me to the master. I was ill there a long time. The many overdrafts on my strength, the exhaustion so often forestalled, evaded, postponed in the preceding months, at last presented their inexorable account, for immediate settlement in full. A period of languor succeeded the crisis of my illness. I lay in bed trying vainly to straighten the tangled skein of remembrance. And all this time I knew no more of my environment than what I saw of the big bedroom and what I remembered of crimson velvet and myriad lustres and reflections. Outside, the season was changing, and with it grew an urgency which either I could not define precisely or chose not to. Sometimes I remembered the huge man dressed in white, and smiled again at his huge bewilderment over my identity and his huge seriousness over my silly question, but I never saw him. I saw only the doctor and servants, and most of the time I was left alone to sleep, or laugh, or cry for some forgotten shame or loss.

Latterly in my convalescence I was judged well enough to sit at the window a little each day, wrapped in woollen shawls and travelling-rugs in a basketwork chair. The sunlight was warm through glass, though they told me the air was cold still. At last I was well enough to go downstairs. Barbered and bathed and dressed in fresh clothes I descended the grand stairs, supported by a servant on one side and supporting myself on the other with a hand on the banister. I was amazed to find my ankle mended – more impressed by that than by my recovery from pneumonia, for the latter had passed in a dream. In what he called the saloon the fat man greeted me. 'Please!' he said, dismissing the servant with a wave and grasping both my arms, 'Do you forgive me for not visiting your sick-room?'

'Of course,' I said. I could not say I had scarcely missed him, when obviously he attached much importance to the point.

'I am so happy. I cannot bear sick-rooms, not even of those I love. Them least of all. But I am so happy to see you well again.'

'I have to thank you for that.'

'Please! No. God has sent you to me in my loneliness.'

'I should tell you at once,' I said, for I saw how the land

lay, 'that I care only for women.'

'Ah well,' he said. 'Some days even God fails me. Only women. You must be lucky in your country. I too might have cared for them, but where are any worth it?' He waved a hand at the countryside, and indeed it didn't look promising. 'I have had to manage as best I could, and God in His infinite mercy knows what the serfs do. I shouldn't say serfs, of course. They've been freed a long time, and are going to be magnified now, and anyway I'm a liberal. But somehow I always call them serfs. Only women. But at least there is conversation, the commerce of minds.'

I couldn't demur at that, having disappointed him once, though the word had unhappy associations for me in Russia. I soon found that just as 'conversation' had been with Captain S a euphemism for interrogation under torture, here it was another name for cards. 'My twin passions, cards and boys, but the cards are always here,' he said. Oh, those weary nights. Oh, those infernal oblongs of pasteboard, with their frowning or simpering faces or, to me, purely blank numbers. Perhaps he saw in the quest for right cards a reflection of his quest for lovers. I can only hope his luck was better in that other line, for at the table it was abysmal, and badly as I played I couldn't help winning. If he or I had taken his I.O.U. seriously, and if my errand had turned another way, I might be a landowner in Russia to this day instead of a storyteller. (On second thoughts perhaps not, in view of subsequent events there.) His play was not improved by a taste for Champagne laced with Chartreuse.

His bulk was in girth more than height. The body was pear-shape, swelling from a bald, rather pointed, head with no visible intermission of neck. He was obviously a pederast, as we called it then – homosexual you say now – and the fact was emphasised by the blouse-like tunic and wide breeches like a skirt of the quasi-military dress he affected. I suspect he painted his face. I grew to like him. He was an overgrown schoolboy of about ten who saw life as a party at which all the best things were either forbidden him before-hand or confiscated too soon, and who grabbed and coveted and lusted with despairing greed. And, d'you know, he bore disappointment better than men who would mock him bear success. I saw in that absurd figure a poise maintained in a world known to be crumbling – and I even learned a little of it; and it stood me in good stead, as you shall hear.

The dogs that got between my feet under the card-table were Borzois. They were the only native thing there, except the man himself presumably. His wines were French, his books were French, his politics were German, being Marx-ian. And his guns were English; I don't know what he paid for them, but I couldn't have afforded them at home, let alone shipment and duty. He was, of course, a bad shot. Not a poor shot, but a bad one – more dangerous to his com-panions than to his quarry. I don't shoot well, but I know when not to shoot. His beaters could marshal the game to give him the best chance, and his keepers could direct their own fire to make his appear better, but nobody could discipline him and so nothing much came of these kind-nesses. No serious wounding occurred while I was there, but it was an occupational hazard for his people.

Dangerous shooting by day and tedious cards by night. All night, often. But there was some actual conversation too. He spoke English well, though whoever had taught him had been excessively polite and it was full of Please. He told me there had been a change of government. (I never heard anybody call it a revolution. That was left to pam-phleteers and journalists in Russia and to enthusiasts of both colours abroad.) The Provisional Government, which had taken office on the Tsar's abdication in March, had been ousted in November by the Bolsheviks, nicknamed Reds. The change wasn't unopposed. Several regions and army groups, nicknamed White, remained loyal to the Pro-visional Government and engaged the attention of the Red armies. The new government pursued the war with Germany, but reluctance was growing in the ranks, Grigor told me, and most people expected that a peace would be made shortly.

I couldn't calculate how this change might affect me or my mission. Other people were paid to take the wide view – to synthesise information, as they liked to call it. I only collected the eggs, for them to scramble. But I could see that if I were caught in Russia after a treaty was signed I might be handed over to the Germans. 'Wait a week or so,' said Grigor. 'The snows will be abating then, and my people shall drive you to Archangel.' That sounded all right. After so much delay another week was nothing. I might still reach Archangel sooner than I should have done alone. And anyway, what could London expect, who stretched not a finger to help me? I was filed in an out-of-the-way pigeonhole and forgotten.

Grigor must have been devoured by curiosity about my purpose in Russia – every thought and emotion devoured him, for five minutes – but he was too courteous to press it. The days passed in a succession of shooting and cards and visits and conversation. The people on whom he called and who called on him – in attempts to help each other through the heavy country hours – made much of me, both as Grigor's friend and as an Englishman. Everything English was fashionable in Russia. Though not so fashionable as anything French, of course. Some of them spoke English. These neighbours were more alarmed than Grigor by political events, but he by his superior knowledge or riches or influence (or merely physical weight, which he could make impressive) subdued their anxieties if not calming them. 'We are a long way from all that,' he said: one couldn't tell whether he meant in miles or moral distance. Courteous again, he always spoke English in company, that I might not feel excluded, and those ignorant of it got whispered translations from their neighbours. Apart from national news, the talk was of horses and harvest, sales and purchase and the increasing desirability of gold coin, and of course the business of death and birth and lust which goes on regardless of politics.

Grigor took a proper part and exercised a proper dominance in all this, but what he really liked was a private gossip with two or three ancient dames, all false hair and real diamonds. He was never so happy as then, nor so much at ease. They would draw chairs closer, and a smile irresistible to himself and others would light his face and he would swell his chest and stretch his thighs, exulting in his existence. In that charmed circle he could forget that he was too fat and too old and that he couldn't do well what he enjoyed doing and that the boys came seldom and briefly. I was not excluded from even this closer circle. He would beckon me, and they would speak English, and a condescending fidget of fans and lorgnettes would be directed at me from time to time. I didn't mind the condescension; their great age entitled them to it, for they were nearly dead. Only anxiety about the bequeathal of their diamonds and eagerness to hear the next episode of local scandal kept them on this earth, I believe. And anyway, these little conversations, like the larger ones, washed over my hearing as a tide that sings you to sleep. So long taut, and allowed suddenly to go slack, I was impervious to the behaviour of others. I was just there, gently smiling, gently talking in my sleep when necessary, gently walking in my sleep in and out with Grigor.

It was his custom to rise late, in an attempt to shorten the day, but I don't know that he wasn't worse off that way, for he always said at our twelve-o'-clock breakfast 'I slept badly. Terrible dreams!' He said it to the room at large, as if expecting the confidential servants to condole with him. But they never did, and I took my cue from them. As for me, I slept soundly; and I couldn't have risen earlier willingly, since he often kept me at cards until dawn, just to make his losses a round number of thousands. None of those country devices for shortening the day worked, individual or communal. They never do. From each the hours slipped out another unexpected way, like quicksilver. But it was all a pleasant dream to me. 'I didn't believe there were still houses like this,' I said.

'There aren't many,' said Grigor. He was like a child in accepting states of mind, and utterances rising from them, which most people would think odd.

'When I was with the gypsies I didn't believe there were any.'

'You must have had a hard time. Sometimes I think that is what I need – a hard time. Then I think I will have a horse saddled at dawn and ride off to find one somewhere.' He spoke as wistfully as other people speak of finding a fortune. 'But I forget and sleep late, and then it's breakfast and then I look forward to a chat with friends and then the cards are ready. And there are people who depend on me. And people I depend on – mistakenly. I'm caught in a web of my own spinning and I never do ride off at dawn. And never shall, you know,' he ended, turning on me a bleak glare of his comedian's eyes as if he'd seen for once revealed the barren country he was condemned to.

I enjoyed our shoots. Not for the sport itself, but for incidental pleasures. The birds, like a handful of darts flung at the sky; the splintering of ice; the terse utterances of the keepers, punctuating silence and shaping disorder; the distant sound of an axe. The farther we went on the estate, the nearer its confines, the better pleased I was. Like a cowardly child safe again in his parents' house, I wanted to see the bullies who had frightened me and mouth defiance at them. But the gypsies had gone for good. I pictured them riding without pause, the dead man still dragged by one foot in the stirrup. I was sorry he wasn't the chief. Awake I pictured them, but surprisingly, I never dreamed of them. We saw no stranger in our farthest excursion. Grigor's estate was vast, and did indeed seem 'a long way from all that'. No sound of artillery, not even an unexpected hoof-beat, contradicted the ordained strokes of his foresters' axes, the scheduled bursts of his keepers' guns. What was prison to him was sanctuary to me.

The snows did appear to be abating, and certainly the ice was cracking. Armfuls of spring flowers were brought into the house – some from its conservatories, some from the warmer regions of South Russia. And with these signs of spring I had a growing sense not of duty (probably, in the way of these things, my mission was no longer relevant, the information unwanted or got from another source) but of England. A wish, soon an obsession, to see the spring flowers there. In particular, to see white and purple crocuses on the bank of a mill-stream that I knew in Kent. An image of those flowers, cool and refreshing, had visited the most feverish moments of my illness. I began to pester Grigor about my departure; and though he regretted the prospect, still he enjoyed planning the journey. It was something new to do, in a fairyland where everything was old. Itineraries were drawn up, lists made, maps consulted. Sometimes he even laid aside his hand of cards, struck by a new idea or doubt; and he would hurry in and out of my room at every stage of dressing as other points assailed him. 'Assailed' is the word. I gathered he had not made such a journey himself this century – city life was tiresome, he said – and he regarded it as hazardous. I don't know what he would have said had he known of the additional hazards peculiar to my case. I didn't breathe a word of them, of course. His mind was so full of brigands and wolves and nihilists and floods and broken bridges that anything else must have burst it.

I was glad I'd not delayed opening the matter, for I saw it wouldn't be accomplished quickly. Just the right sleigh must be found, and overhauled. Just the right horses must be chosen and relieved of their present work and fed-up for the ordeal. Just the right men. And there was the question of provisions and armament, and of striking a nice balance between need and weight. I didn't lose sight, in the absurdity of this excessive fuss, of his immense kindness in doing so much for a stranger. I knew that were our positions reversed, I should not do so much, nor so gaily, for him. And I despised him for doing it, as one does despise superiorities. Yet I saw it was well done.

When all was ready physically, still he would not sanction my departure until he knew the state of the country north of us. And this was not easily learned. His estates were wide. The estates of his neighbours were wide. He and his neighbours moved in prescribed orbits. Travellers from beyond were few; news from beyond was merely rumour, and that got at fourth or fifth hand through channels not discoverable, let alone reliable. The newspapers were less trustworthy than the banknotes, which is saying something. So we began a series of reconnaissances. I had whetted his appetite for novelty. We would rise not at dawn, admittedly, but considerably before noon and eat a standing breakfast – though it was as large and luxurious as usual, so the standing was merely an inconvenient and useless gesture. Then with a large party of armed retainers we would ride north, beyond the boundary of his lands.

We didn't see much for our pains. Little bands of deserters, who kept well clear of us and regarded Grigor's benevolence and inquiries with equal distrust. The railway line, but never a train. A few farm people, who belonged to him in some degree, I suppose, and seemed surprised to see him so far from home, and apparently uttered blessings of questionable worth and lamentations of obscure reference and never, by any chance, knew what was happening between there and Archangel. They seemed, so far as I could judge, to think Grigor's curiosity about a place so distant impious and ill-advised. But he was cheered by seeing them, and by their seeing him so adventurous, and what with his simple joy in these meetings and his frequent recourse to a pocket flask he often forgot our purpose in having come so far, and returned home triumphant in the mere fact of it. I didn't remind him. I saw no need of elaborate reconnaissance anyway, and to remind him would further postpone my going. Finally, the next full moon was agreed as the date of departure. He said it would be both lucky and useful. 'In the meantime,' he said, 'I will write to my wife.'

'I didn't know you were married.'

'We married to please our relatives, and we live apart to please ourselves. So everybody is pleased. She will tell me the state of the country. If she ever gets the letter.' All those wolves and brigands and nihilists and floods and broken bridges were vivid to him again, so he sent the letter by courier, and still doubted its arriving. 'I can't send my best courier,' he explained. 'Because I don't want to lose him as well as the letter.'

I asked him once 'Do many nobles live in this region?' It sounded like one of those ridiculous questions you see in foreign-phrase-books, so of course he took it seriously. I was thinking of the Countess I'd heard of. But he said there had been only one, old, Countess and that she had gone to Moscow and died. He spoke as if the two actions were synonymous. In nineteen hundred and five. I was sad to leave Russia without learning the identity of that shadowy figure which had somehow encouraged me at the start of my escape. She must remain among the unrealised possibilities which characterise that land. Sometimes it looked, under its snows, like a blank sheet of paper waiting for somebody to write on it a decisive word. And for all its upheavals, it still looks like that to me. Many have been confident to make that mark; and the snows have received its fleeting impress and absorbed it and obliterated it.

So I counted out the days to full moon and watched local society as you would watch a puppet play, removed from them both by language and by the listlessness of convalescence. They too, I thought, really lived at a distance from their immediate experience and action. The old dead women lived in the vicarious vitality of diamonds. And they had a distance of years to escape into, too. Even the young women

88

– there were some, despite Grigor's strictures, who could still compete with their jewels – were living at a distance. Youth limited them to a distance of wistfulness; they hadn't yet bought that vista of years, paying for each stage of it in flesh. I watched them, as they watched each other with mingled envy and disgust. I studied them immune, like a scientist at a microscope. I was never 'a ladies' man' even at home. One woman at a time, yes. That's different, elemental, like riding a horse into the dawn. The other's a party accomplishment, too self-conscious to be real. I had more to do with the men. The men were friendly. They thought I could teach them something they needed to know. They thought every foreigner could. They wore amazing watch-chains, and rattled coins in their pockets, and were more aware of literature and art than their English counterparts, and asked my opinion – and were given it, of course – on matters I knew nothing of. They were friendly and none of them asked what I was doing in Russia and I flowered in their company, though it was a forced flowering. 'I see you too have a low opinion of our women,' said Grigor with gloomy satisfaction as we were driven home after one of these parties.

'Not at all. But I shan't be here long. And they all seem pre-occupied.'

'The young ones are worried about their dowries and the old ones are worried about their wills and the matrons are worried about their daughters.'

I nodded. And I remembered the bird singing in its cage and the crumbled coat-of-arms, and I wished. And I remembered my cousin Gloria, and I wondered. And these are pleasant to do when you're twenty and a little tipsy and the night air blows cold in your face and life still seems a gallery of pretty pictures from which you may pick. I thought myself a realist. I had indeed lived dangerously for some months, but that doesn't make a realist. The lesson is no good without the pupil, and I had to experience a lot more, among less obvious realities, before I was ready to learn. But I thought myself a hard, tough, clear-sighted fellow. Youth needs arrogance, for it has no achievement.

And so I crossed off more of the days before full moon. No letter had been received from Grigor's wife, but he did not make its receipt a condition of my going. It was simply another anxiety for his collection. The sleigh was now ready – nailed and oiled and painted and varnished and whatever else they do to sleighs. He did tell me, but I've forgotten. It was wrought to perfection and had a curiously fragile look as if another touch would break it. The chosen horses were produced and shown off. I wished the two horses that had carried me this far to safety could have drawn the sleigh, but dismissed the wish as neither hard nor tough nor clear-sighted. Provisions and equipment and armaments were piled in the hall and solemnly weighed and examined; and the men who were to accompany me were quite dazed by Grigor's instructions. Just as well he wasn't given to travel himself, I thought. The household could hardly have borne this strain more than once.

The round of visiting was increased to mark my departure – that desperate little society seized any pretext for celebration – and we played cards longer for higher stakes. And Grigor drank more than was good for him and grew tearful; and I drank more than was good for me and grew boastful; and glasses were smashed and shots fired at the ceiling and awful vows made; and neither of us could remember what it had been about next morning.

I can't say I was exactly sorry to be leaving Grigor's house – it had been only a hospital to me – yet there's a kind of regret in closing any episode; I suppose because each such closure, however unimportant or even welcome in itself, is a rehearsal of the final one. I took to rising earlier in order to linger round the house and grounds before Grigor was up, touching things or gazing at them almost sentimentally. It was not the act of that hard, tough, clear-sighted youngster I wished to impress on the world and myself; but the world was not there to see, and you can't always fool yourself. Few days remained. I tried to wring from them their essence. Faint and sickly-sweet it seemed, like the scent of the spring flowers which showed pale by day and paler still beneath the waxing moon. Those days and nights – one drifted into the other imperceptibly, without conventional division – were marked for me by a sense of equilibrium. I felt strangely irresponsible, like a child on a swing whom anybody's hand can push either way. I felt I might be carried toward England in Grigor's sleigh or somehow carried back to the girl in the town, equally without my volition and without my really caring. It was only an effect of illness, I suppose, but the strange environment made it stranger.

Grigor, learning that I liked the folk-tales of his country, summoned to the house some nights those of his people who were famed for telling them, and appointed himself interpreter, appearing to enjoy the occasion as much as I. The tellers, perhaps because they were old, perhaps because it was the proper manner, spoke slowly, with dramatic pauses, so Grigor had plenty of time to find the nicest translation. Rapt in both the excitement of the story and the duties of relaying it, he was at his most endearing. When the storytellers had been dismissed, each with a gold coin clenched in fist to see them safe through the troll-haunted dark, Grigor would try to repeat their performance complete with gestures and expressions, but he was prevented by a shyness which lived surprisingly in his exuberance, and had to be content with recapitulating the happiest moments and smiling or crying over them. Some nights the peasants would come to make music, reminding me of my night at the girl's house. Grigor threw himself into this entertainment, too, accompanying them, unskilfully and inappropriately, on a grand piano – foreign, of course – and making its candles jump and tearing its frilled silk in his excitement. Sometimes the music would take a spiral form, like my snow-storm, whirling twin strains of passion and sadness to an unbearable height from which performers and the listener's senses would drop exhausted. The music seemed to rise into these ecstasies of itself, without the direction of the players, who could only accompany its wilfulness, marvelling at it and themselves. Night after night I listened with eyes shut or watched with ears covered, trying to detect the slightest move by any of them to command it, but I never could. I can only suppose it was an outburst by influence and traditions of which they were unconscious agents. And Grigor was as subject to this spell, if not so deft in helping it, as any of them – lifted off the ground as easily and sooner, and more reluctant to fall again. Listening to those melodies, you could believe the old stories of men bewitched by music to their utter loss and harm.

Grigor's neighbours didn't join us at these entertainments. They preferred their music sophisticated by Europe. This was too raw for them, too eloquent, perhaps, of passions which had lately found less harmonious expression in the capital. A few bars of this might have burned the diamonds and withered the flesh – that or turned them to new uses. So Grigor and I were the only grandees present. I don't know how grand I was, but his grandeur was enough to cover us both.

Amid these novelties I didn't quite forget the General and his Cossacks. I could not suppose they had forgotten me – the poster was a contrary proof – but certainly they had lost the scent. I was safe in Grigor's fairyland of jewels that must be sold and bosoms that must be bought. Grigor, with one wave of his great arm, would brush away the Cossacks as he had brushed away the gypsies. Swathed in all the furs of Muscovy, guarded by giants, I should be drawn through air by a fury of horses and jubilation of bells, scarce touching the snow which once had terrorised me, leaving the Cossacks below baying at the full moon like outwitted wolves. Grigor, marvellous Grigor! Whom I would have embraced in gratitude but for his inconvenient tastes. I wanted to give him a present or do him a service. But he had every object he desired; and what service could anyone do him, bar cause him hardship or relieve him of his wife? Neither was quite in my line. I could only stifle my yawns at the card-table.

He'd had a gallery which ran the length of the house fitted up for target-practice, and there I fired away some mornings, the detonations competing with the strokes of an axe in the woods as if I'd made a wager that I would shoot an army before somebody else could fell a forest. To my chagrin, I found that my shooting at a target never approached the shooting I'd done under stress. Perhaps I needed the stimulus of danger; perhaps it was the different revolver. Grigor came sometimes to watch, wearing ear-plugs to keep out the noise. I supposed he must wear them when shooting out-of-doors, though because of his flapped hat I'd never seen them, and that they rather than pride made him heedless of instruction.

Still no letter came from his wife. 'I pray she's well,' he said. 'If not, I might be expected to go to the city, and I should hate that.'

'You could come part of the way with me.'

'Even so I should hate it, my dear.'

He tried other ways of getting a report on the state of the country between us and Archangel, but unsuccessfully. It seemed a waste of time. I should see the state of the country soon enough; and in the political and military turmoil to-day's best report might be useless or worse tomorrow. Grigor kept saying, 'If only the railway weren't out of action,' and then saying, 'But perhaps you'll be safer by road,' and eating another sweet or lighting another cigarette or ringing for more tea to comfort himself.

I can't describe the ambiguity of my feelings. I didn't care whether I went home or back into Russia, yet I dreaded venturing outside the safety of Grigor's house. In sudden fright I nearly said 'I've changed my mind. Let me stay'. But if I began wishing it, he might stop. I'd seen enough of his temperament to know he wanted only what was withheld. And if I flinched from danger once I might never be able to face it again. And I wanted to be active, feeling that action was the key to my being and that only in action could I integrate those qualities in me which warred or went rotten in idleness. It's a confusion I've suffered since, but never so badly as then; and whether it was a symptom of lingering illness or returning vigour I still can't decide.

It was the dream time, neither winter nor spring, neither boyhood nor manhood, that comes to all and is the seed of our best fruition throughout life. Don't begrudge me my dream time, nor my lingering in recollection of it. I had nobody to share it, remember. And anyway the dream time is short enough, the waking comes soon enough, to please the most grudging.

The dream wasn't absolute. Though I wouldn't say so, I too was worried by the prolonged absence of the courier. I never admitted the possibility of Grigor's wife being ill – or harmed, although she lived in Petrograd. I related everything to myself. The courier's absence must mean dangerous roads. Grigor's anxiety showed itself in more religious observance, or at least reference, than usual and a flow of forgetful endearments in addressing me. I suppose he sometimes confused me with the posturing young men who looked darkly from photographs everywhere. Everywhere. On the piano, on the mantelpiece, on many tables made for that purpose and many not. You couldn't judge their relative importance to him from the frames, which were all silver and uniform; and the difference in size might depend on the donor's estimate of their relation rather than Grigor's. But they changed places periodically, and I suspected a clue there, for I believed Grigor rearranged them himself. The piano seemed the place of honour. He could see it from his usual chair, and I suppose that when he played he was serenading his favourite of the moment. He had no photograph in his bedroom. Only ikons. All the photographs were old. I didn't suppose their subjects looked quite like that any more; and probably the warmth of their feelings had cooled, just as the ink of the inscriptions had faded.

He received many letters, though, and spent some portion of each day at his writing-desk, getting very inky there, and enclosed bank notes. These enclosures may have indicated blackmail or simply kindness. It was hard to say where one ended and the other began in his complex affairs. His man of business was often with him, small and worried. Most of the men in closest attendance on him were small, as if, taking warning from himself, he had a pathetic faith in the competence of small men. I suppose he spent money faster than his estates made it. Without an heir, he saw no fun in enriching his wife. As the steward pulled a longer face Grigor smiled more, until he grew cross and blustered and dismissed the man, throwing bills after him.

Perhaps he really would have liked to exhaust his fortune, to get to the bottom of riches and see what was there, but his patrimony was so vast that the task of substantially reducing it defeated even his ingenuities of extravagance. If only that optimistic energy had been put to a worthy, or even a constant, work. Instead it was dissipated among unreliable affections and spasmodic enterprises. There he sat, flashing rubied fingers, passing a hand over his pomaded remnant of hair, smiling and weeping and talking. And one day he would be summoned before his God, or at least before a tribunal of the gold-framed saints who encircled his sleep, to account for his use of millions of roubles. Or so he believed, which is the same in effect.

I write of him at length because of the many people I met in Russia he was the only one I knew, or at least had an opportunity of knowing. And because Russia has printed itself in my memory, a growing enigma, I try to read some clue in Grigor, who was at once the most and the least characteristic of her sons. He must have died long ago. He was a good thirty years my senior. I know the stories of centenarians in Georgia, but he wasn't a Georgian. Anyway he was too obvious a target for the new regime – too rich, too lukewarm a socialist, 'nice' to his serfs, too aware of the West. I don't know what happened to him and I don't wish to. I prefer to remember him as he was then. Whatever happened afterwards was irrelevant. Almost certainly it would have provided the hardship he sought, and possibly he found in it a semblance of salvation. I don't fancy he would have lasted long in a labour camp; but I can believe he might have lit his end by some act of kindness or even heroism. So he may have realised his dream of riding out at dawn.

I say Russia is a growing enigma to me. At the time it was only the scene of my adventure, and might as well have been anywhere else. But as I've grown older, away from it, it has grown more vivid to my imagination and more obscure to my intelligence. My eye, trained to hold for life what it saw a moment, reproduces pictures of Russia, pictures of places I hurried through and people I left behind – an album for which I must find the captions. Like one of the newspaper competitions you see, though I don't know what the prize can be. Peace, perhaps, Russia exorcised at last. No, that is not possible; for I left my youth there and my thoughts will wing back to it till the end. Perhaps everyone who tells a story is a revenant, returning either to get rid of an experience or get to grips with it, somehow get the better of it. Alter it, probably.

I dwell on this uneventful period in the country because I want you to share my experience as nearly as you can, and this dream time is important to the whole. So the languid months must be represented, in a true account, by pages without incident, and you must bear them. But there is an end. The ice is cracking, the snows are abating, the moon is waxing, the flowers are fuller; and unseen forces, accidental and deliberate, already converge.

The conventional division of days, and of each from its night, seemed latterly to collapse. Whether we did indeed sleep all day and stay up all night. I can't say, but I know the lamps seemed always to be lit. Whether I was so accustomed to be drunk by then that it seemed sobriety, or whether my irresolute languor began to resemble drunkenness, again I can't say. I was lost in Grigor's fairyland, where the glitter of an icy lake we shot across would dissolve without warning into the glitter of diamonds on a breast that cushioned or fingers that counselled; and again, before I could enjoy or heed, into the glitter of lustres on a chandelier above my solitary bed. The subdued accents and sparing syllables of the keepers would be transposed into one of Grigor's rhapsodies. The handfuls of darts that became birds in the air fell under our fire to become wolves or Cossacks on the ground; gypsy faces peered from among branches; my own wanted face was on every card I turned up; all these disguises and transformations marked by the inconsequence of dream, by a delightful sense of immunity. I must suppose I was drinking too much, or that the irregular hours and pursuits, unsuited to a convalescent, had caused some mild recurrence of feverishness. Perhaps my mind had paid toll on the long roads as well as my body. Perhaps I was simply learning the Russian view of life, being initiated into the world Grigor inhabited; perhaps their wonderful fairy tales were plain statements of fact. Actual or fantasy – and I did bring back one or two souvenirs of fairyland – I was glad it happened and glad it didn't last long. It didn't agree with me. There was nobody I could ask. I could only shut myself in the shooting-gallery and try to blast some common sense into the situation.

One day Grigor came there to tell me that a Red officer, a cousin of his wife, had arrived, who had travelled some of the road I must go. I went down to the saloon and found Captain S.

PART TWO

VIII

We advanced toward each other from opposite ends of the long, shadowy, tessellated room.

'You are like death, Captain,' I said. 'I have come so far to escape you, only to find you at the end.'

Normally he would have replied to this literary conceit, but now he stood silent. He did indeed 'look like death', in the popular phrase. His face was pale, his uniform not immaculate. Small as he had looked in the cells of the fortress, he looked smaller here, shrivelled. Had it been summer I should have thought him troubled by the dust of the roads, for he licked his lips and cleared his throat more than once before saying 'The position has changed. I am travelling with a warrant for the General's arrest.'

'How did you know I was here? Did Grigor—?'

'I didn't know. I came at his wife's request, to give him a first-hand account of the state of the roads. Also because this is one of the few decent houses on my route.'

'I suppose the General's to be court-martialled for letting me escape.'

He sat before replying. I understood him to murmur 'Can we sit down?' Grigor wasn't in a hurry to appear. Perhaps he disliked this emissary of his wife.

'A man was caught after your escape,' said Captain S, in the tones of one talking in his sleep.

'Mikhail?'

'Mikhail?' He dragged the name from far beyond his immediate concerns. 'Oh. No. Not Mikhail. A farm worker. He was found in incriminating circumstances. In a bolted stable.'

'But, good heavens, it was bolted on the outside.'

'Possibly. If he wasn't a fugitive, he was arguably an accomplice, for a horse was missing.'

'Accomplice? I'd never seen him in my life before.'

'No? You won't see him again, either. He was shot and buried under your name,' – so, taking his horse I had taken his life – 'and a report forwarded to G.H.Q. It was unlikely, you see, that they would send anybody to investigate.' He nearly smiled, appearing to relish and be revived by this instance of professional cunning. 'But it's not because of that innocent deception that I have a warrant for the General's arrest. You may have heard there's been a change of government. He has chosen to remain on the wrong side. Can one get anything to drink here?'

'You can ring the bell. It's beside you.' I wouldn't have moved to help him had he been dying of thirst in a desert. I could hardly speak to him. I walked to a window, to wash my eyes of him. Was it to keep him in a job that the people were hungry, the armies retreating, the lands lying waste? He was pale and anxious not in any turmoil of conscience but because he was afraid he hadn't changed sides soon enough and afraid he might fail in this first assignment. I knew nothing of the rights and wrongs. Red and White were no more to me than two armies of chessmen. But I knew one piece the game would be better without.

I thought so fiercely in those terms that I saw them written on the landscape before turning to watch him given his drink and refusing one myself. 'So I've nothing to fear?' I said. 'I'm officially dead? And the government that ordered my arrest is gone?'

Again he licked his lips and tried to swallow that persistent dust before saying, 'That's right.' But it wasn't right. I remembered the poster. The General would not advertise my escape; and the Reds could know of my survival only from Captain S. They would be as curious about a British agent as the others. The Captain appeared to be travelling alone, and a General is not easily arrested in the midst of his troops. Uncertain of getting him, Captain S might see me as a providential 'bird in the hand'.

'It's amusing that we should meet at the Countess's,' he said.

'Which Countess?'

'Grigor. We call him the Countess behind his back. You can't have failed to notice his tastes. At least to notice them?'

'I didn't know he was a noble.'

'He doesn't flourish the title now. He didn't before, to give him his due. But he was careful to keep it. Like the money he's always lamenting.' Comparing his pay with his cousin's husband's superfluous fortune, Captain S sounded like a spiteful wasp that had got into these gilded and marbled saloons. 'You remember my speaking of him? I always said you'd have common ground.'

'He seems in no hurry to see you.'

'His wife stands between us. I like them both, and try to help them, so of course each suspects me of favouring the other. Amusing.' He didn't sound amused. He had fallen into a new range of experience that disconcerted him. I wondered who 'we' were who called Grigor 'Countess' behind his back; and I wondered what we called his wife behind hers.

Grigor joined us. 'I was just saying what a good fellow you are,' said the Captain. His cousin's husband nodded ambiguously. 'But that you always think I side with your wife.'

'It was good of her to send you. It was good of you to come.'

'And this is your friend who must travel to Archangel? We've met before.' Grigor looked at me as if told of a sickness I'd suffered. 'We enjoyed many discussions about the works of the English novelist Dickens. But you don't read him, do you, dear old fellow?'

'I've heard of him,' said Grigor. He looked like some slow heavy animal goaded by a smaller and quicker. He had the same resentful consciousness of his own defects. I hoped he might turn on his tormentor and rend him, but they continued talking trivially.

The deadly cold that had possessed me at sight of the Captain now passed. His footing was more perilous than mine, and our meeting unluckier for him than me. He was alone with his warrant. He was an untried and probably untrusted recruit to the Reds. He dare not depart from his orders even to capture a spy, and he couldn't get permission because communications had broken down. And if he turned his back on me I might settle accounts.

'Will you stay the night?' I heard Grigor ask.

'Please. But no longer. I'm on duty.'

I thought Grigor was relieved by the limitation. He went out on the pretext of having a room prepared. I wondered whether I should follow and tell him the truth, but I wasn't sure enough of his response. I reckoned Grigor's evident dislike would prevent the Captain from telling him. If I reckoned wrongly, I must handle the consequence when it happened. Of course I could have taken a horse and made good my escape before I was missed, but I had temporarily lost the power of simple action. I suppose the terrible Russian lethargy had overcome me. And I would rather have the Captain in front of me where I could see what he was doing than at my back. I returned to the shooting-gallery and resumed practice. During that time, and afterwards while reading in my room, I heard and saw nothing of the others; and when I went downstairs again in the late afternoon the saloon was deserted. But a bright fire and steaming samovar indicated that Grigor was expected for the rites of tea. Probably he was taking Captain S over the estate. I dropped into a deep armchair to wait for them.

A conservatory stood against the windows of the room. The arrangement made a pretty effect, but the plants excluded much of the light. The room was shady even at midday, and by late afternoon, before lamps were lit, it was mysterious, the plants making green what little light they let through and the tiles of the floor, great lozenges of black or white marble, dully reflecting it so that one had an illusion of floating on water. The crimson sofa where I'd once lain was a single blaze of colour. I often wondered whether it marked a brief rebellion by Grigor against the decorators' scheme or was a sign of his wife's swift passage, a feather dropped in her flight to climes more congenial.

Grigor and the Captain came in. I couldn't read their faces, but I didn't think they were any better friends. Nothing significant was said over tea. There was little conversation even of a formal kind. Each of us was lost in his own thoughts. I could not guess Grigor's. Presumably he was reminded of his wife by this visitor. Though most of his moods were effervescent, I suspected that the true griefs never rose to the surface. Tea done, we drifted apart without having really come together and left the Borzois in possession of the hearth.

Lying in my bath I could hear the Captain splashing in his, next door; and while dressing I could hear him dressing and losing studs and dropping hair-brushes. These proofs of our common humanity didn't disarm me. I kept the door locked and my revolver within reach.

At first dinner was as awkward as tea had been. Worse, since we sat closer and felt bound to talk. And though wine loosened our tongues the antagonisms remained. Afterwards we played cards. At midnight I said I must go to bed. Perhaps Captain S believed I was escaping. Perhaps he couldn't endure the idea of leaving at daybreak, as he said he must, without having laid hands on me. Anyway, as I rose from the table he spoke to Grigor in Russian.

'In the presence of an English guest I can't understand you,' said Grigor, who was reckoning the score.

The Captain then said, 'This man is a British spy. I interrogated him in prison, from which he subsequently escaped. I order you to assist me in his arrest.'

Grigor, with only a second's pause, continued to count. I stood, my hand still on my chair, entranced. Captain S began to repeat his words more loudly. Grigor interrupted him, saying, 'I did not hear you. Because, my dear, if I heard you, my having sheltered such a guest might be made to look like complicity.'

'My superiors will regard failure to help as active resistance,' said the Captain quietly.

'I know you are not threatening me,' said Grigor, 'because it would not pay you. But if you were, I would remind you that your superiors are a long way off, that you have still to execute your warrant on the General and return safely to them, and that my word is law over a wide region here.'

Captain S rose, steadying himself with a hand on the table – like us, he was a little drunk – and strode from the room.

'I must go after him before he can get help or send a message,' I said. 'May I take a horse?'

'Take the sleigh. It can be ready in a few minutes.'

'I might lose him in that time. And a horse can go where a sleigh can't.'

'Take the best, then. I'll come with you.' Ringing for servants and not waiting for them he snatched the lamp from the table, where the cards still lay as we'd played them, and we hurried to the stables, men running to us in the hall and bringing coats and other necessities after us as Grigor bade them. The wind nearly extinguished the lamp in our short walk in the open, but he sheltered it in his coat.

The groom who'd helped Captain S was still closing the doors when we reached the stable, and we could hear hoofbeats, little in the night. Inside, the smell of hay and oats assaulted us. Draughts made the lamp flame flicker wildly and our shadows danced all round us. The horses, wide-eyed and startled at this unusual waking, seemed to share our sense of urgency. Grigor picked the best – he was, oddly, a good judge of things he couldn't use well – and in a moment

106

I was leaning from the saddle to shake hands with him. Even in my hurry I was touched by his initiating this English gesture. 'Will you come back afterwards?' he asked.

'No. Whatever happens I must go on now.'

By this time he was nearly running to keep up with me, while servants tried to put his fur coat on. 'Is it true?' he panted. 'What he said.'

'Yes.'

'How exciting! My dear, how exciting!' Now he abandoned the attempt to keep pace and the men were at last able to get his arms in the coat sleeves.

'I can never thank you enough,' I cried.

'God speed you.'

That was my last glimpse of him – still struggling with his coat, characteristically absurd and kind together.

I gave the horse his rein, and nervous excitement moved him as quickly as I could wish. Once in the saddle, I was my own man again. Doubts and dalliance fell away like dreams at waking. The fact of my being for a change the pursuer enlivened me. Perhaps the clean air was best stimulant of all; I seemed to have breathed for months only cigarette smoke and scent.

Now I fixed my attention on those other hoofbeats, small beyond my own. I must hold them with all my strength and draw them closer. Captain S was a meticulous man. He would allow himself only the hours before daybreak for his attempt to get help or send a message : then he would resume his journey to the fortress. I didn't know how near he might find soldiers of his side, or a telegraph still working. I was back in the familiar yet daunting vastness of night and snow, where probabilities could not be measured. But I was a veteran of it, and he was not.

Those other hoofbeats, little but distinct – he was keeping to the road – were like a glittering minnow in an ocean of darkness. But it wasn't really dark. There were the stars; there were the heads of a forest outlined against them; there,

107

growing clearer every minute, were all the landmarks of my map. All strange to him. And behind him the terror of pursuit. For he must guess, even if he didn't hear. Ah, I would have made it yet more terrible if I could, to repay him: for mocking Grigor no less than for torturing me. The restraints of the house were left in the house. Even if it weren't a matter of saving my life, still I would kill him when I caught him now. And he must know that. He must know that the man behind him in the night was no less a beast of prey for reading Dickens' novels; just as I had known it of the man in the next room who dropped his collar stud under the dressing-table. And he dare not kill me. I was wanted alive.

I chuckled, remembering Grigor's manner at the card-table. He hadn't liked being ordered by a man so notably his inferior not only in rank but in humanity. But I mustn't let my thoughts wander. I must keep them fixed on the Captain. In his desperate errand he had put himself at precisely that disadvantage I had dreaded: he had let me get behind him, where he couldn't see what I was doing. Of course he might lead me into an ambush; but I kept a wary eye on the shadows and luminosities of the night. I kept my hearing alert, too, for any change of speed or weight in the other horse's hoofbeats that would indicate its rider had leapt off. But there was no such change. That ruse was too much a gamble for the Captain, if he thought of it.

Our horses were evenly matched and the distance between us remained constant. The night passed. I knew its textures and scents and stirrings, although the change of season had altered them. The eastern sky was lightening, and still the Captain's horse drummed the roads. He must turn soon. Unless he'd become obsessed with the idea of recapturing me. Now the sun was making its first signals over the roof of the forest, and I could see the Captain. A touch of white in the dark figure showed he had turned his face to see me. I drew my revolver from its holster. I didn't know its effective range, but I would try a shot. The ground sloped upward. I would hold my fire until I reached the top. But there I saw what stayed my hand.

Ahead of us lay the railway, which I'd forgotten, and on it, about to cross our path, was a train crowded with Tsarist soldiers. As I reined in, wondering whether I should retreat beyond rifle-shot, Captain S spurred his horse to leap the track only a few feet in front of the oncoming engine. I couldn't help admiring the act. He got his reward. He was safe on the other side, while I was held back by the inordinate length of that inordinately slow train. I heard no firing. Presumably they thought a solitary Red not worth the expenditure of cartridges. The men on my side of the train pressed to the windows to see me. In time – a long time – the last carriage passed and I was able to continue.

Captain S was out of sight. I knew, as if I'd been told, that he had abandoned himself to his obsession at the expense of his duty. He was riding to Archangel, to make sure I should be stopped there.

About mid-day, reaching the northern boundary of a plain, I found myself among trees that were merely a windbreak for a village which lay on the bank of a river below. I might get breakfast here. I tied my horse to a tree. The Reds would be looking for a man on horseback, and possibly hadn't much useful description beyond that. I debated whether I should be less conspicuous without Grigor's fur coat. You may think there was no question, but remember that underneath I wore the evening dress he'd given me – a singularly ill fit although the legs and sleeves had been lengthened and the waist gathered in. On the whole I reckoned I should be safer keeping the fur coat, which was at least reasonable wear for the time of day. I transferred my revolver from holster to pocket and set off down the slope, slipping on fallen cones and stumbling over concealed roots.

The village street extended not an inch beyond the last house. What I dignify under the name of street was in fact

no more than a way of trodden earth, except where enter-
prising cottagers had improved their frontage by the intro-
duction of stones. It appeared a poor community. I wondered how best I should go about getting food. It wasn't a
place to find an eating-house. I knocked at the nearest door.
With my knuckles. Knockers were beyond the village's
means or ambitions. Waiting for answer I stared about me
and missed, not for the first time, the touch of any bright
colour. A square inch of red would have blazed like a forest
fire in that sombre land. The plumage of the girl's singing
bird and the upholstery of Grigor's sofa were the only bright
colours I could recall seeing in Russia.

These thoughts were interrupted by the opening of the
door. An old woman held it open, with every sign of a readiness to slam it shut again. I performed my pantomime of
having been struck mute and deaf by the fire of enemies or
the misfire of my own rifle – I never determined which; but
she was an unresponsive spectator, taking the tale of my
troubles, as old people often do, merely as a cue to relate her
own, which she did at length regardless of my professed in-
ability to hear. I had no need to feign incomprehension, and
was free to peer over her shoulder into the house, speculat-
ing on what hospitality might follow. I should have earned
breakfast when I'd borne her lament to its end. When she
stopped, more for want of breath than matter, I signified my
hunger and tried to insinuate myself into the gap between
door and jamb. Whereat she slammed the door in my face
with an energy I shouldn't have credited her with.

A little out of countenance from this defeat, I continued
along the street. I must use more forceful pleas if I was to
fill my belly. The street ended in an open space, from which
several alleys led off and at the centre of which stood a
pump. I wondered whether I'd been foolish in leaving my
horse available to any thief and visible to any pursuer while
I sought food in this inhospitable place. I saw approaching
me along one of the alleys the dark figures, featureless be-

cause the sun was behind them, of women bringing buckets to the pump. I stood watching their approach, the sun displaying me to their scrutiny as it obscured them from mine. Down the narrow way they swooped, like birds to water, their fluttering clothes and the utensils they carried giving them strange shapes, their talk echoed and multiplied by the high walls they walked between. I stood waiting them, uncertain whether I was prey or predator. The sunlight was warm on my face and I could hear, quietly persistent among the women's strident cries, a gentle sound of water within the pump behind me. It was a moment of immeasurable tranquility, of improbable equilibrium, untouched by danger past or impending. I felt I had stood thus for ever awaiting the women come to get water, as if we were figures in a picture, our relation eternally unresolved. Next moment the thing broke; the women were nearer and I was nervous again. The group split to pass me, staring and smiling and shouting still, and continued to the pump where they began their task, still with backward glances. Well, nothing for it – I must repeat my wounded veteran act. It sickened me more each time, with thoughts of the many men who were in the condition I feigned. But the deceit was forced on me by the same war which inflicted their wounds, and I was no more to blame than they. Nor any less. We are all guilty of war and what it does to us.

So I mimed the wounds I had never suffered and the hunger I suffered indeed. And the group about the pump, timeless themselves, stopped in their work to watch my timeless dumbshow. Women getting water have watched men tell of war since the beginning. I can recall the scene in detail: the distribution of light and shadow on ground and figures, the mouth of the pump still dribbling water because a woman had not completely released the handle. I can see the pump and the shallow basin about its base and the low coping of stone that had crumbled in places. And the women, arrested in various postures, all looking at me. The tale I told cannot have been new to them, but I suppose their days were blank enough to give it distinction.

When I'd finished they looked at me still, but now with a sympathetic relaxation of face and manner, and then turned inward in conference, darting glances at me to make sure I awaited their decision. I did await it, of course. I'd nothing else to do. Besides, I was enchanted. One of them, appointed to speak or anyway assuming that office, stepped forward and indicated that I should follow her. The others grinned, but their mirth was more kindly than ribald. She led me back along the alley she'd come by; but instead of going to a house, as I expected, we passed out of the village – it was only a few strides – as far as a spinney on the river bank. There she made signs that I should wait, lying hidden, and that she would return with victuals.

From my hiding-place I could see straight across the square and along the street beyond to that other spinney where my horse stood. The view was deserted, the women having dispersed, so that the horse and I were at opposite ends of a perspective. And as I watched, powerless as in a dream, I saw a posse of riders come into the little picture of horse and trees that was framed by the far end of the street. While I wondered which way to run the woman returned carrying a covered basket. I pointed to the scene that was taking place. She comprehended it in a glance and obviously set her wits to devising an escape for me. (I sensed that she was practised in such exercise. I dare say village life gives a young woman opportunities of intrigue.) She took my arm. I still started at the touch of a fellow creature : my experiences at the fortress had done that for me. She led me at a run into the village and through a house and into a yard behind it where a horse was stabled.

I recognised the horse. It belonged to Captain S. Bewildered, I could only stare. My companion urged me into the saddle and thrust the basket of provisions into my hand when I was there. I obeyed and accepted and automatically guided the horse through the gate that was opened for me; but I scarcely remembered to wave goodbye and thanks. To be astride my enemy's horse and not know where that enemy was nor why his horse was given me – this was a situation I couldn't grasp. I examined the saddle and accoutrements for a clue, but all was in good order, telling no tale of surprise or death. He must have found faster transport, possibly leaving the horse in payment.

The lane we rode took us through wooded ground parallel with the river. I glanced behind me. No chase. My pursuers would not expect me to be mounted so quickly. Probably they were searching the houses. I relied on the old woman to delay them a good time. I'd come out of my scrape better than I deserved. The swift resumption of pursuit reminded me that I was hunted, and would be hunted until I was out of Russia.

It was a fine morning for a gallop, the sun warm and the river sparkling where the breeze shaped it into nuggets. With my basket I looked like a baker on his round. A baker pilfering his own stock, too; for once clear of the village I thrust a hand among the provisions and began a lucky-dip breakfast. I turned north again, urging the horse to its utmost.

Glancing back I could still see the village; and now I saw issue from it, at a speed which distance could not disguise, several riders. To escape I must set an unbridgeable barrier between us or hide. The latter I disliked, and the landscape offered small hope of the other. The time of day – broad noon – made my situation worse. You can usually fashion some ruse of the dark, but what advantage could I pluck from this hour, too empty and too bright?

My backward glances had distracted me from my environs. Now I saw that the woodland had thickened on either hand and that these two walls converged, forcing me inevitably toward a gate that was guarded by a man with a gun. Possibly it led into private ground. I hadn't time to speculate. The man challenged me and, I not halting, raised the gun to his shoulder. Too late. I'd fired already. At that range I couldn't miss. And in that hurry I couldn't choose my mark nicely. His gun flung wide in a last convulsive action, he was relieved of his post for ever. Cursing this necessity, I was about to leap the gate when I got a better idea. The closing woods and a dip of the ground hid me from my pursuers. Quickly dismounting, I bade the horse kneel and hauled the dead man into the saddle. I tied his arms about the horse's neck, urged the horse up again, tied the man's boots in the stirrups, opened the gate and whipped this grim fellowship onward, where soon they must be in full view of my enemies. The corpse fell all ways, of course, but it stayed on so long as I could see and at a distance its attitudes might be mistaken for those of exhaustion. Carrying my basket on my arm, the ownerless gun over my shoulder and my pistol in the other hand, I hid myself deep among the trees. Some few minutes later the first of the riders – on Grigor's horse – swept past my peep-hole, followed at an interval by the rest. They gave no glance to right or left, obviously deceived by the imposture ahead.

IX

I plunged farther into the trees. The dead man's gun was a burden, but it was safer in my grasp than thrown away where the enemy might find it. Besides, I should be glad of extra fire-power if I had to stand and fight. Thinking so, I ejected the spent cartridge from my revolver and inserted a fresh one. The bill for liberty was growing long – the farm-hand shot in my place, Mikhail probably dead one way or another, and now this fellow, whose only offence was that he'd tried to stop me when I hadn't time to argue.

With each hand full of potential death and with accomplished death heavy on my conscience, I broke and trampled a way through the gentle green of that spring forest, where the life that rose in swelling bud and joyous bird seemed to rebuke me. I listened for the return of the riders, stopping now and then to hear better, but there was no news of them. The Captain's horse, affrighted by its burden, must be leading them still.

I walked until dark, when the slender moon showed me a hut. No sign of occupation. I crept nearer this wooden box as if it might burst apart to loose death on me. And indeed it might. Stillness, silence. Well, if enemies were lurking inside better see them than turn my back. The door opened easily to my hand and moonlight showed me the hut was empty. I suppose so few people came there that the owner saw no need to lock it. Mind you, it had nothing to attract a thief, nor any but a desperate traveller. Damp, mildewed, in bad repair, obviously it was not a dwelling but merely a shelter for woodcutters or sportsmen, and had been allowed to rot from even that lesser requirement. But it was the best lodging I was likely to find. I lay down among the dead leaves and live beetles and slept. Of course it was foolish. If I were telling you the proceedings of a wise man I should have no story to tell, for a wise man would never have set foot on my mission.

Lacking a groundsheet, I could not expect to find this an easy couch, and I slept badly. I don't know whether fungus gives off harmful fumes – certainly it gave off an evil stench – but I suffered horrible dreams. A dozen times in the night I rose, removed the bar of broken wood I'd put across the door and went outside, to shake off the dreams and to allay the unease they'd left with me. I saw no cause for alarm. Each time I thought the starred sky and open air a bedroom more wholesome than the one I'd chosen. A dozen times I nearly resumed my journey, only to decide I'd have another shot at sleeping soundly. In the end I must have succeeded too well – and I must also have grown careless in replacing the bar – for on my last waking two men had hold of me. They weren't in uniform, and I couldn't tell their calling by their dress. One of them had my gun. I always unbuckled it when I slept, for fear of shooting myself. Well, I thought, they're not soldiers, so probably they regard me as a mere trespasser. They bound me and took me outside and put me in a pony-drawn sleigh. It was a very different article from Grigor's – more like the things I'd made as a boy. The moon was paling in a blue sky. Probably they were taking me to a magistrate, who would impose a fine or so many strokes of the knout; though it struck me unpleasantly that they hadn't once addressed me.

We travelled most of that day, my captors taking turns to drive and to guard me. Despite the discomfort of my bonds, I fell asleep in the luxury of being a passenger, and woke, and drowsed again. After dark we entered a considerable town and went to its barracks. My hope of being regarded as a trespasser dwindled. I was taken before an officer who spoke English. He was an elderly man, tired, whose brusque manner masked a distaste for his work, I thought. I could imagine him kindly in private.

'You are a British agent,' he said. He held a copy of the poster, and a razor would make short work of any denial, so I said nothing.

'Why were you sent here?'

'To incite your soldiers against peace negotiations with Germany.'

'You speak Russian?'

'No.'

'Then how could you incite Russian soldiers?'

'I had helpers in Russia.'

'Name them.'

'A man called Mikhail. I never knew his other names.'

He consulted a paper on his desk. 'Who else?'

'Captain S.'

He looked at me expressionless, and spoke to a civilian who sat beside him before asking, 'If that were so, why should he give you up?'

'To divert suspicion from himself, I suppose. Or possibly he's changing sides again. I believe he has a history of it.'

'He interrogated you when you were first arrested last year.'

'That was to both our advantages. I mean he could save me from the shooting-squad on the pretext of needing more time or silence me if I threatened to unmask him.'

'But he didn't appoint himself to interrogate you.'

'No. I dare say the General appointed him.'

'Are you saying the General is in your country's pay?'

'I was never told so. But I believe that after my escape he pretended I had been caught and shot.'

He consulted his papers again and looked at me unhappily. He would rather have been smoking a pipe at home, I thought. The civilian sat watching with undisguised enjoyment, like a man at a play. The twist I'd given the conversation had been unpremeditated. Initially I had been simply buying time, because time is hope. Then I had seen that

117

though I couldn't help myself I might harm my enemy. He had thought to stop me at a distance, but by this accusation I might draw him back to me; and when we were face to face I would manage somehow to kill him.

'You will go with this gentleman,' said the officer, indicating the civilian. Who rose, gathering himself together into his good clothes with relief and reluctance, exactly as one does at curtain fall. He led the way and two soldiers with rifles escorted me behind him. A motor-car stood in the barrack yard – a thing still rare enough to be exciting.

'You were lying, of course,' said the civilian as we were driven away. He spoke English with a German accent. A settlement with Germany must be imminent, if not accomplished, and the fate I'd dreaded had fallen on me. 'These Russians are fools. I always know when a man is lying.'

'Do you always know when a man is telling the truth?'

'No, but that happens seldom enough for the deficiency not to matter.'

We were driven to a railway station. Like the town we'd passed through, it was 'blacked out'. I couldn't understand why, since the war was ended. An armoured train stood at the platform. I was led aboard it and into an opulent compartment. Railway carriages in eastern Europe then were still furnished to resemble not so much a private carriage as a private drawing-room. Buttoned leather upholstery, curtains, tassels, tables, lamps, all contributed to the illusion that what the window showed was a picture in an album idly turned, or an image projected by magic lantern. But this window showed nothing. There were steel shutters outside. Handcuffed, I sat opposite the German while the guards took up their posts in the corridor. 'We shall have plenty of time for talk,' he said. 'All the way to the Fatherland. To civilisation, Beethoven and Goethe. I have always said we Germans and British have so much in common that war between us is a tragedy. It is nothing less than a war of brothers. But these Russians are barbarians – mystic when

118

they're not stupid, alien to us both. I'm glad to see the last of them.'

'Why is the station blacked-out?'

For a moment I thought Beethoven and Goethe didn't know why. Or perhaps he was deploring my prosaic interests. Then he said, 'They have turned from shooting us to shooting each other.'

The train moved off. I studied my companion with interest. Having spent the war spying on our allies, I was glad of a chance to see one of the enemy. Everything about him twinkled – pince-nez, discreet watch chain, glossy boots, and more than all his smile, which he wore like a badge. I believe he was cultivating a sense of humour. Earnestly. I suppose he'd graduated as high as he could go in a sense of art. 'Now every mile is a good mile,' he said.

Food and coffee were brought in on trays, and my hands were freed so I could eat. Lamps lit and curtains drawn, the compartment was a jolly place. It was warm too. The train increased speed. Probably the driver was German, and shared my captor's eagerness to be home. The intelligence officer, for such I took him to be, poured brandy for us both from a pocket flask. It made me sleepy. I rested my head against the comfortable leather. 'Take a nap,' he said. 'We've plenty of time.' I shut my eyes. The loosing of my hands had given me no immediate advantage, for the guards kept close watch. I could ask to go to the lavatory, and try to hurl myself from a door on the way. I would try it in a minute, when my head was clearer. Then I slept.

Years or minutes later I was woken by the lurching of the train. It alarmed me, as things do at waking in a strange place, and I wasn't calmed by seeing that the German had stopped smiling. 'Is it safe?' I asked fatuously, like a timid old lady. I was answered by an even wilder lurching, which shook us from end to end of our seats and then forward into each other's arms. A loud dull roar of collision or explosion, and the train stopped. The succeeding silence was filled after a minute by a sound I recognised, sweet to me then as birdsong at summer dawn. It was machine-gun fire. I didn't know who was firing or why, but in effect they were my best friends. 'Barbarians,' said the German. The guards had taken defensive stance in the corridor, their rifles thrust through slits made for that purpose in the shutters. All along the train a sporadic rifle fire was audible, answered in contemptuous bursts by the machine-gun outside. A train official came running along the corridor and spoke to the German, repeating a phrase and gesturing toward the front of the train. The German shrugged and scowled and pulled on his greatcoat. 'The engine has been derailed by terrorists,' he said. 'We must get out before they blow up the rest of the train.'

We alighted into the night air that still held the coldness of winter while offering a promise of spring. It smelt of cordite too and hot metal. German and Bolshevik soldiers were tumbling from other doors and opening fire toward the front of the train, where the ambush must be. For the moment my guards stayed with me, but I had hopes. The night was dark, lit only by a dim glow seeping into it from the open doors of the train and by an irregular glare ahead where the derailed engine had caught fire, perhaps, or perhaps had set fire to the undergrowth by flinging wide its hot coals. Otherwise there were only rifle flashes and the deadly white lines of machine-gun bullets. The soldiers from the train had been formed into two parties, and now set off in different directions in an attempt to attack the machine-gunners from behind. A Red officer ordered my guards to join the advance. The German told them to stay. They hesitated, then ran at their officer's repeated order. Two foreign civilians were nothing to them.

'I think we part here,' I said. 'I hope you reach the Fatherland safely.'

He wasn't armed, and he was a slight man, and he was a realist. 'Perhaps we shall meet in happier days,' he said.

I stumbled into the darkness, away from the firing, which soon I could hear only by turning my head and listening carefully. I was now reduced to exactly the condition I'd been in on first escaping. No horse, no gun, and lost. I might have collapsed under this reversal had I not been borne up by a belief that so many escapes must be the work of a saving hand. I don't mean I got religious. I never did. But I had a sense of some process which would preserve me for later use. So I ran, stumbling, almost gaily into the night. I could no longer catch any sound of the fighting. I ran back along the railway, my boots crunching the small stones it was laid on. Then I reckoned I might be safer off it, in case reinforcements came by train, so I ran on rough ground parallel with the track but at some distance from it. I'd no plan. The railway would lead me back to the town, but I'd no idea how far it was, having lost count of time while I slept. They wouldn't be pleased to see me there. The picture of my intruding on the officer's domestic retreat – I had a fixed impression of him with pipe and slippers and probably a cat – made me laugh. I laughed alone in the darkness. Laughing to oneself is considered a sign of mental weakness, as bad as talking to oneself, but both habits kept me sane, I believe, in those months.

My run soon fell into a walk. I'd put enough distance between me and the train. No good in exhausting myself. So I walked on with a regular stride, and whistled and thought better of it, and was able to see a few faint stars. Under Grigor's greatcoat I still wore the tailed evening coat he'd given me. And over the evening trousers I'd pulled riding boots. Altogether I was a ridiculous figure, like a scarecrow broken loose. What must I do next? Nothing simpler. Steal a horse. I'd stolen two. I could do it in my sleep. But why a horse? Why not a motor-car? The one which had taken us to the railway station had been left there, I believed, for I seemed to remember the chauffeur boarding the train with us. I had not driven a motor-car – except once for a few minutes when a friend of the family had taken us for a spin – but it looked a fairly simple business. I knew they had a bad reputation – 'dangerous contraptions' and less reliable than the horse whose power they boasted tenfold – but so long as they went they went fast. The boldness of the plan attracted me. Given a choice of courses I always took the boldest. Because it was often the safest. In this instance I was the last person the Reds would expect to walk into the station yard, even if they knew of the train's derailment, so I was safer doing that than doing other things ostensibly more cautious. And the plan had a simplicity which had often proved lucky for me.

A little play-acting might help. I began to think of myself as a Russian landowner (eccentric, of course, for only an eccentric would wear such clothes) who had been for a stroll in the country and was now returning to reclaim his motor-car. Not exactly Grigor – I hadn't the physical attributes for that role – but somebody like him. I borrowed some of his insouciance to go with the borrowed clothes and practised his masterful gestures, ready to put aside any question or protest.

I hadn't slept on the train so long as I'd supposed, for soon I saw the town. The black-out wasn't absolute, but only a few privileged lights burned there and I recognised it more by its silhouette against the sky. No sound of pursuit. Perhaps the fighting continued. Perhaps the Reds had been annihilated. Perhaps they were busy routing the terrorists. I didn't care which, so long as news of my escape didn't precede me, so long as the German intelligence officer twinkled elsewhere with Goethe and Beethoven and his chosen luminaries. It was pretty certain that no news of the ambush had got back, for no reinforcements issued from the town.

Encouraged by seeing my goal, I walked more briskly, and soon the railway sidings and the station loomed large. Walk with authority, I told myself. Eccentric Russian landowner. Along the track, clambering with difficulty onto the platform, and across the station. There was none of a station's normal bustle. Only a few officials and soldiers stood at the row of arches which separated the platforms from the street outside. The ordinary service was suspended, I guessed, and the railway available only to military trains.

The officials watched me as I walked toward them across the deserted platform, my boots ringing on the stone. I made them ring as valiantly as I could, needing all the encouragement music can give. I'd have had a drum-and-fife band march with me if I could. Bar this song of steel on stone the station was silent. Until my noisy tread woke pigeons that lived in the high roof and that flapped about to find a new resting place. Most big railway stations have a cathedral look, being expressions of their architects' only real religion, and this Russian station was the most cathedral-like I'd been in. Partly because of its desertion, I suppose. The officials stood like affronted priests as I strutted toward them purposefully but not hurriedly. I took my time so as to appear in control and have a chance of practising under my breath the phrase I'd heard on the train, which I took to be 'White terrorists'. Nearing the officials I pointed dramatically back the way I'd come, exclaimed what I trusted was 'White terrorists' and made with hands and voice an imitation of an explosion. Their questions I shrugged and waved off, as I'd seen Grigor do, and left them to tackle the thing as they chose. The news had distracted their attention from me satisfactorily and I was free to saunter through the arch and into the yard. The motor-car was still there.

I should say every idler in the town had come to look at it. To steal it, given half a chance, judging by their furtive appearance. But I wasn't going to stand for anything like that. I wondered whether the station lamps, hooded but lit, or the presence of two armed sentries at the station entrance had restrained the thieves so far. Whatever the cause, they only stood and looked. Not every face was covetous. Many hadn't strength or hope enough to covet, but merely gazed at this symbol of the unattainable. They looked like the crowd that used to gather outside a society wedding or an opera house to watch the rich go in and out.

The two sentries ran into the station, probably summoned to go to the help of their ambushed comrades. I mustn't stand there. Hesitation is too revealing, and lets courage trickle away. I walked to the motor-car and climbed into the driving seat. There was a stir in the crowd, an exhalation of pent breath. But not an actual movement, nor a formal utterance. There weren't many controls that I could see, but those few looked terrifyingly mysterious. I'd no notion of how to start the thing. I tugged ineffectually at one or two levers. In doing so I noticed on the floor an iron bar, bent twice at a right-angle, and I remembered hearing talk of something called a starting-handle – and even seeing one in strenuous use. As I recalled, it had to be inserted at the front of the engine and turned, maniacally, desperately, cursingly.

Some of the crowd had sidled closer, and were watching me with a dangerous mixture of envy and doubt. They reminded me of the wolves. I would give them something else to think about. I threw the starting-handle at the feet of the nearest and indicated with an angry shout that he should crank the engine. He was a big, surly brute, as likely to brain me with it, I thought. But another, who obviously had some acquaintance with the mechanics of internal combustion, took the handle and did what I wished. His puny strength wasn't equal to the task; whereupon his fellows joined him and all worked with a will in relays of two. There's a lot of loose energy in a crowd, that can be turned to any use you please – if you seize it first, before the crowd gets its own ideas. And in any Russian crowd there was still a big balance of servility to be drawn on, no matter who the drawer so he found the traditional note of arrogance. By this time the entire unemployed and criminal population of the town was engaged in starting my motor-car, envy and doubt forgotten because I had given them something to do.

At last the engine woke, with an alarming noise, and my volunteer mechanics leapt back to safety. All except the first of them, the little man who'd really done nothing but set an example. He remained, in heroic posture, proudly regarding his handiwork. I wished I had something to give them. Thrusting my hands into my pockets – unaccountably I'd not done it till then – I found as if by magic several coins. Gold coins. They must be part of the largesse Grigor habitually carried for such purposes. It was a marvel they'd remained there throughout my journey and capture. I separated some for a reserve, slipping them into an inner pocket. The rest I kept ready. Doing this surreptitiously, for the crowd wasn't one I would tempt. I released the brake, after a moment of searching for it, and managed with an effort to turn the motor-car so its nose, or bonnet, pointed to the town. Having turned, I held it with the brake a moment and threw my handful of coins to the crowd. The men rushed on them in a silence more expressive than any shout, falling and fighting in their eagerness but all without a word: words were luxuries they could no longer afford. The gold coins jumping on the cobbles, the frenzied movement of the crowd, the clatter of pigeons woken again, the Byzantine pretensions of the railway station that stood aloof from these disturbances, rising as by right among the stars – I was aware of all these for a moment. Then I released the power of my motor-car and was hurled into the town.

All other questions were temporarily excluded by the urgent question of how to manage the contraption. Its power was frightening, and I had only a hit-or-miss command of the controls. My career as a motorist was likely to end in killing somebody or smashing something. It would be grimly amusing if I were arrested and imprisoned for such an offence. Luckily there was little traffic of any kind in the town, and my vehicle must have carried an 'open sesame' sign, a military registration perhaps, for more than once a sentry or policeman assisted my passage – though there was no need in streets so quiet – and saluted. I wondered whether I should pass the officer who had consigned me to Germany, but he was safe indoors, spared the waking nightmare of seeing me again. I drove through the last gate, again assisted and saluted by sentries. The town stopped abruptly, as towns there seemed to, with no straggle of suburbs, and I was in the countryside once more – a countryside unlit and apparently unpeopled.

It looked innocent under the newly risen moon. But only as a map looks innocent – because divorced from what it represents. I mustn't forget that forces deliberate and accidental were ever active against me. I mustn't fall into the old fallacy of the tossed coin. The odds would be no more in my favour next time because I had escaped so often. Each danger was a new toss-up, and the odds were fifty-fifty. It was mathematics. Hope and fear were superstition. I was just a coin tossed innumerable times. The only extraneous factor was that I might be worn out in the process.

Thinking of coins, I remembered Grigor's. I don't know how a young fellow would get on today in such an adventure. Certainly he would have more technical aids than I had. Probably he would have more technical knowledge and skills – I was a preposterous embodiment of ignorance and arrogance. But it's unlikely he would have the joy of holding a fistful of gold coins and jingling them to hear their tune. I didn't jingle them for long, though. The motor-car demanded both hands and full attention. The only part of it I could operate with any confidence of success was its loud hooter.

It chugged and exploded, slowed and leapt, on into the night, a little world of glass and metal moving through the sky. The sky was more apparent than the road, being better lighted. Which way to Archangel? I didn't know how to guide myself by the stars, so I must wait for the sun to direct me. And I mustn't run out of fuel. I'd seen a spare can on the running-board, but I didn't know where to pour it and I

126

didn't know how to get more when that was spent. Snow had begun to fall again. Or fly, rather, for it came level at the windscreen, in hard pellets, and I blinked instinctively, forgetting the glass. The driving-seat had no protection but a windscreen, while the passenger compartment was snugly boxed and glassed in. I would pull in somewhere and make myself comfortable for the night. That was wiser than wasting fuel on a wrong road. In time I found a gap in the embankment of the road, where a gate opened into a field. I turned off the road, and by dint of moving every control to the opposite position managed to stop the engine.

I felt lost. Not in location, I mean, but in identity. I suppose a youngster's never sure of his identity, and has to make do with activity; but my case was aggravated by the violent changes of circumstance, mood and assumed persona. Falling asleep or waking, I often wasn't sure whether I was a holy man, a wounded soldier, a whimsical landowner or a British agent. None sounded more or less likely than the others. The only things in me I could affirm with certainty were sensations. I could say I was tired, I was cold, I was hungry, I was afraid. But I couldn't say who I was. I shut myself in the passenger compartment, which was warm and smelt of leather, wrapped Grigor's coat round me and fell asleep, relying on daybreak to be my alarm clock. It was the best sleep I'd had in a long time. No consciousness of present discomfort or future danger obtruded on it. Like the engine, my mind was switched off.

I woke to see the first rays of sun coming level across a ploughed field and causing the frosted crest of each ridge to glitter so that the field resembled a frozen sea. The sky was palest blue. Little patches of ice crackled under my feet as I stamped about to ease the cramp in my legs. And in sheer joy of being alive, and free, and answerable to no one, I sought more frozen puddles and danced on those too. This satisfactory rite performed, I grew a shade more sober, recalling talk among pioneer motorists of engines 'freezing up'.

I wasn't sure what it meant, but this seemed a likely place and likely weather for it. I was right. I got no response from the engine to any of the switches, nor to my frenzied cranking. Equal to ten horses it might be, but they were ten dead horses now and merely ten times more exhausting to flog. I threw the starting-handle down in disgust – its cold iron had burned and blistered my hands – and wondered what to do next. I might have known what to do with an ailing horse, but this thing was a mystery. I'd heard those same pioneers speak of boiling water got from a cottage or farmhouse, but where was I to get boiling water? And how ask for it? And anyway, what did one do with the boiling water? I must abandon the motor-car, which had at least sheltered me for the night, and walk.

I walked briskly northward. Somehow Grigor's coat on my back and Grigor's coins in my pockets made me feel invulnerable. 'Walk with bags of swank,' the drill-sergeant had used to say. And I did that morning. I was a Russian landowner, I told myself, a stranded motorist, sure of people's respectful help. I'm walking with bags of swank across Russia, Sergeant. 'Less of your lip,' he would say. 'Keep your eyes to the front,' he would say. 'I'm no beauty. Don't look at me.' So I kept my eyes on the paling moon and the glittering furrows, and heard the ice still break under my tread. A ploughed field meant a farm somewhere near, I reckoned. And a farm meant breakfast. Half an hour's walking brought me within sight of a low straggle of buildings. No men or beasts to be seen, but smoke was rising from a chimney. My money or one of my impersonations would get me breakfast. Gaily across the yard I strode, ice jingling at my heels like spurs, and through the open door as if invited and into the kitchen. Where at a long table before the fire several White officers sat at breakfast.

X

The sight of them was so unexpected that the smile of pleased anticipation remained on my face, and I stood a moment paralysed, unable to adjust to the situation, while they looked up at me. When my mind resumed its function my first thought was that they would need to keep better watch if they were to survive long. I even began to tell them so before remembering that the advice wasn't much use in English. It was apparent that none of them spoke English, but they recognised it – or perhaps only the accent. They rose with smiles of enlightenment and took my arm and clapped me on the shoulder and indicated I should join them at their meal. I was among friends.

Well, England was an ally of the Provisional Government to which these men remained loyal, so they would naturally welcome an Englishman. Not so much because they relished war with Germany, perhaps – though there was a professional pride among some of the officers that kept them at it after the private soldiers had wearied – as because they might hope for English help in fighting the Reds. I reckoned I could eat breakfast in safety. Between mouthfuls I stole looks at my companions, trying to read in their faces some sign of their response to the recent upheavals, but there was nothing beyond an enjoyment of the moment, a voracious appetite for the hot food and drink set before us. No doubt the facts of the political and military situation were pigeon-holed in their memories, but hot coffee and fried eggs engaged their consciousness, made their eyes brighten and their faces smile. I looked at them more carefully when my hunger and thirst were assuaged. They were clean and well barbered, their boots perfectly polished and their uniforms exact. Perhaps their gaiety was a little nervous, a degree tightly strung, the high spirits which possess men, even men habitually morose, in a climate of risk. I've seen the same thing round a gaming-table where the stakes were high – though not so often as in battle : men are more solemn about losing their money than losing their lives.

Breakfast finished – and nothing was left – chairs were turned to the fire, legs stretched and cigarettes lit. Conversation began, in strict order of seniority, quiet at first but soon noisy. They made jovial attempts to include me, with gestures and clownish faces, but they couldn't raise a word of English among them. I must try my bad French. 'Je veux un cheval,' I said. They laughed, politely, as if they thought I was making a joke. 'Sérieusement,' I said, 'il faut que je vais au Nord. Vitement. Pour la patrie.' Then they rose as one man and took me to the stables. The White armies always had horses. Perhaps they'd have done better if their strategic thinking had not been seated so firmly in the saddle, for the Reds, notable for neither horsemanship nor horses, more than balanced that inadequacy by their use of mechanised transport and weapons. The machine-gun I'd heard chattering of death across the derailed train must have been one of the few the Whites had. Or more likely the ambushers had been one of those guerrilla bands which throughout the civil war attached themselves to either side, or fought both, at whim.

Anyway, we were standing in the stable, presumably discussing which horse I was to have, when a peasant came in and addressed the senior officer. Probably the farmer himself, I thought, for he was dressed better than the labourers I'd seen. Whatever he had to say, speaking urgently but in a low voice and pointing outside more than once, seemed important enough to interrupt our business. It seemed also to concern me somehow, for faces were turned to me during the man's narrative, with expressions less friendly. I held myself ready for trouble. Any news about me could only be bad. My career in Russia had not been of the kind that wins friends.

The farmer led us outside. In the yard, a horse harnessed to it, stood the motor-car. And obviously the insignia on the front told my new friends that it was a military vehicle of their enemies. Two of them held my arms, while others, indicating the motor-car, asked angry questions of me, forgetting my ignorance of their language. Then they turned their questions into French. I won't trouble you with more examples of my bad grammar, but I conveyed that I had stolen the motor-car. My statement didn't appear to convince them. They discussed it doubtfully, in strict order of seniority. The two fellows who held me, being the most junior there, said nothing, but gripped my arms tighter to show their devotion to duty. Next my pockets were turned out. There was nothing but Grigor's gold coins; and those, after being examined with surprise, were returned to me punctiliously. I carried no papers – not even the requisite ones of identity now, for those neat forgeries, the pride of an elderly craftsman in London, had been confiscated on my arrest. Everything important – the information culled at some cost – was undocumented, as you know. They took off my heavy overcoat to find the tailor's label; but that, I suppose, showed only Grigor's name, probably unknown here, and his tailor's address. Anyway, the coat too was returned to me. It was all very polite. The courtesy of Russia could be excessive by English standards. But also it could end abruptly, turn into savagery with no warning transition, and that might happen at any minute.

We all trooped back to the farmhouse kitchen, my arms held again by the mutely enthusiastic lieutenants. In that weather warmth took priority. Presumably my nationality was in my favour. I mean there was no apparent reason for an Englishman to help the Reds now they had embraced Germany. But knowledge of foreigners is usually scant and assessment of motives difficult. I had entered White territory in a Red motor-car, and that was enough to warrant questioning. The senior officer stared at me, stroking his chin, a slight frown drawing his eyebrows together. He had been cut, or had cut himself, in shaving, I noticed. Probably he was meticulous to the point of hurting himself in his duty too. I tried to look back at him frankly and forthright, but that attempt inevitably has a dishonest air. He spoke to one of the lieutenants, who went out and did not return for a long time. I guessed a message had been sent, requesting advice or help. It was some comfort that the secret police now served only the Bolsheviks.

After a delay embarrassing to everybody an armoured car stopped outside the farm. In it were the young lieutenant and several sailors. I couldn't imagine what sailors were doing so far from the sea. I was put firmly but not roughly into the back seat, between two young sailors who looked so very stern that I guessed it was the only way they could stop themselves grinning, and away we went into the morning, our speed somewhat reduced by the motor-car I'd stolen, which was towed by ours, presumably as evidence against me.

By now the sun was as high and strong as it would be that day, but the pools and ridges of ice remained. It was a pretty day for a drive. The territory we were crossing gave more evidence of military activity than I'd yet seen. Obviously the civil war was being prosecuted more vigorously here than the ordinary one had been. There was no sign of fighting, but every sign of readiness for it. We passed several patrols, and guard posts manned equally by soldiers and sailors. The armoured car jolted on over frozen roads and frozen fields impartially. The terrain was flat, sparsely wooded, with farmhouses. It was the kind of landscape that makes you think there must be sea just beyond it, just beyond that glittering edge. I knew from my recollection of Grigor's maps that there wasn't, but wistfulness and the presence of sailors and the glittering horizon combined to maintain the illusion. I remembered the excitement, nearly unbearable, with which I'd approached the sea as a child, bouncing in a pony-trap from the Welsh railway station, desiring and dreading the moment when somebody would say 'You can smell the sea now. Take a good lungful of it.' Those rides seemed as improbable now as this one would have seemed then. But no; the small boy would have accepted it without question. Of course he would be taken prisoner by White Russians and driven in an armoured car across their country. Such things are a boy's familiar climate. The adult too soon loses faith. Already, only twenty, I could hardly believe in the boy in the pony-trap going to the seaside. But he would have believed in me.

We stopped at a gate, the towed vehicle bumping into the back of ours. An avenue led from the gate to a house standing among trees. I guessed that I'd been brought to a headquarters for further interrogation. After a brief parley between my escort and the guard, sailors again, who turned out from the lodge to look at me, the gate was opened and we proceeded up the avenue. More guards on the ornate steps of the house. I was helped down, courtesy still prevailing, and led inside.

The house had been requisitioned, I guessed – its elegance a bit damaged by military occupation, its peace broken by the self-important bustle of adjutants with those mysterious papers which adjutants always carry. The adjutants looked at me and hurried on, as adjutants do. When God created adjutants, they looked at Him and hurried on. We stood waiting in the hall, from which a wide staircase spiralled up, a chandelier hanging in its well like a frozen fountain. Boots rang on the uncarpeted stairs and inquisitive faces looked over the banister as the paper-bearers hurried up and down. The machinery of command was working all-out here. Perhaps in every war more men have borne documents than arms, and perhaps the fact has always bewildered the minority. My escort of sailors stood waiting patiently, but I saw no reason to stand, and sat myself on one of the gilt and silk chairs. I would make the most of the courtesy while it lasted. After a long delay we were summoned upward, exalted to the presence of the commanding officer.

I didn't distinguish him at first among the group who awaited me in a drawing-room, because he wore civilian clothes. Somebody presented me to him, calling him Admiral. I thought the mufti ominous. It looked like a readiness for get-away. But perhaps it only signalled his divorce from the sea. He had the kind of eyes called 'penetrating' – though they're more often a symptom of fear or optical disease. He was impeccably dressed. A frock coat that might have been new from the tailor that morning; a silk tie secured by a pearl-headed pin; a high, glossily starched collar; geometric trousers. He was shaved faultlessly. His dark hair, with a few white strands, was cut short. I reckoned him intelligent, indecisive and inclined to bad temper. I wasn't sure that the combination of those qualities would win a war, but certainly he would win a 'best-dressed admiral' competition. He motioned me to a chair beside the fire and took one opposite. His staff stood at a respectful distance, as if expecting a demonstration of Mesmerism. Perhaps he practised it. Certainly he'd fixed his 'penetrating' gaze on me again. Or perhaps he fancied himself a good judge of men. The unsociable often do; and something in his deportment suggested he wasn't at ease in the company of his fellows. This suspicion rather endeared him to me. I wondered how he'd been lured off the lonely ship's-bridge and persuaded to take command of a land operation. He addressed me in French. He had an impediment in his speech, and he gabbled and drawled alternately in an attempt to govern it. I answered that I didn't understand, that he spoke too quickly. His impatience didn't allow him to speak more slowly. Instead he called an aide to his side who acted as interpreter.

'The Admiral says you are surprisingly young.'

It's not a remark you can answer, so I didn't. If that was the high-water mark of the Admiral's sagacity we weren't going to get far.

'The Admiral does not believe you are a Bolshevik, but would like to know how you got the motor-car.'

'I stole it.'

'Where?' We were getting down to business now, superfluous phrases omitted.

'From a railway station. I don't know its name.'

'What were you doing there?'

'I'd been arrested by the Reds and handed over for deportation to Germany. But the train was ambushed and derailed.' This news caused a pleased excitement. They chattered among themselves like an aviary when bread's thrown in.

'In the confusion I escaped, walked back to the town and took the motor-car.' This, to my chagrin, fell as an anticlimax.

'Were the soldiers on the train killed?'

'I don't know. They were still fighting when I left.' More discussion. The Admiral took little part in it, only watching irritably and waving his hand. When the talk dwindled he resumed his questioning, looking neither at me nor the interpreter, but gazing into the fire as if that might consume falsehood and leave the requisite truth.

'What were you doing before you were arrested?'

'I was a guest of Count Grigor Smirnov on his estate.' The Admiral raised his eyes from the fire to my face a moment. I fancied that the rank rather than the name had impressed him. His gaze dropped to the coals again, but no question followed. The interpreter waited, puzzled but trying to appear confident, like an umpire at a game where the ball has vanished.

'He gave me the clothes I'm wearing,' I said, seeking to follow up my advantage.

'The Admiral didn't suppose they were made for you.'

135

The others had tittered already, so I didn't feel obliged to contribute. The Admiral looked up slyly to see how I'd taken it.

'The Admiral finds your answers so far satisfactory, but wishes you to remain his guest while further inquiries are made.'

'Of course.' I bowed. The Admiral bowed – only his head – and walked out, followed by his staff. Only the interpreter remained with me. I wondered what inquiry would be made. Grigor would vouch for me, and the Admiral hadn't access to the files of the secret police. I looked safe enough.

'How long will the inquiries take?'

'Impossible to say. Things are not normal, as you may have noticed, and communication is slow. How are things in England?'

'I haven't been there for some time.'

'You don't have the Germans on your soil, of course. That makes a difference.'

'Will you go on fighting them?'

'If they remain here. In places they're helping the Bolsheviks.'

An adjutant came in and spoke to my companion, who then led me to my quarters. They were small enough – in the attic of the house – and had previously been servants' rooms I guessed; but they had been refurnished more comfortably and bore signs of hasty and incomplete vacation by another occupant, probably one of the Admiral's staff. Left alone there I stared through the slanted window and thought about escape. I wasn't on parole and the house didn't appear strongly guarded. I was still pondering this when I was again summoned to the Admiral's presence. In his study this time. It was a sparsely furnished room, the chief contents being a big desk, empty, and a big map on the wall.

'The Admiral wishes you to know that you are of only minor interest to him' – nobody likes being of minor interest

– 'but that he is famous for his attention to detail. "No detail escapes him", in your English phrase, so please do not try to be the exception.' I wondered whether the Admiral was the author of these playful variations on his theme. 'If his inquiries are satisfactory, he will help you on your way. If you try to forestall them, he will have you shot. Neither is important to him. And on that understanding he invites you to dine with him.' All very brisk and seamanlike.

It was lucky I was wearing tails, for dinner was a formal affair, with fine glass and silver and napery. It began early and lasted long, running through many courses and wines. And all the time an armed guard – a Tartar, I believe – stood behind the Admiral. These were dangerous days, and men can't be read like charts.

Toward the end of the meal, when I'd lost count of the wines, red, yellow and green, and of most other things, an adjutant hurried in and spoke to the Admiral, who made a grimace of annoyance as if told of an accident in the kitchen. Then he addressed the company, who rose with varied expressions of alarm or excitement. 'Red cavalry is reported in the area,' said the interpreter. 'It will take time to call up reinforcements. Meanwhile we must garrison the house.' Well, I'd done most things in this war. I supposed I could turn my hand to helping one lot of Russians fight another.

'What shall I do?' I said.

The interpreter conveyed my question to the Admiral and relayed the answer 'Stay in your quarters'.

'I'm not very good at that. Can't I fire a rifle or carry a message?'

But the Admiral had gone. Well, if they didn't want my help they couldn't complain at my helping myself. I went to my room to get my outdoor clothes. While I was pulling them on I heard the ground reverberate under the hoofs of cavalry, and a moment later the first shots were fired. The household must have been outnumbered and ill-managed, for when I stepped onto the landing the attackers were already in the hall below. The defenders who stood their ground were dealt with summarily and the Reds came up the stairs, driving a few of the Admiral's staff before them at sword point. They appeared to have no guns. Probably they'd thrown them down without stopping to reload. And that was lucky for me. I had seen already how I must go down. I must go down the chain which held the chandelier, trusting it would hold me too.

As the fight neared me I put my legs over the banister, grabbed the chain and let my weight pull me down. The gauntlets Grigor had given me were of stout leather, but the speed of my fall and the tightness of my grip caused the chain to cut through them. My boots hit that lovely cascade of crystal drops, shattering and scattering it, and I floundered there a moment like a salmon at a waterfall. I didn't pause to admire the resemblance. The Reds were still engaged with the retreating sailors, but they could hardly have failed to see my descent. Fortunately they didn't know who I was; otherwise they might have given me special attention. The hall was empty, the attackers having rushed upstairs or into the rooms that led off it. The front door was open and my way clear. I ran down the steps and along the drive.

The night was moonless. All around me I heard shouting, the clash of steel, an occasional shot, but I met nobody. The lodge was deserted. The gate had been broken down. On the road, tethered and unattended, stood a row of horses. Patiently they stood, though a little restless under the noise. I'd no time to pick the best, even if I'd had light to see by. I clambered onto the nearest and urged it to a gallop.

I'd kept my wits alert enough on the ride from the farmhouse to know now where the north was, and I hurled myself toward it. Another road must have lain parallel with mine and higher, on the other side of the White headquarters, and I saw there the headlights of an armoured column making speed. The Reds might regret their housebreaking soon.

I passed no traffic or traveller on my road, and I was not pursued. I was mounted again, and I determined not to be unhorsed this side of Archangel. I was at home again, in the familiar dark. I was back among realities – stars that glowed and dimmed, trees that stood or passed, to the tune of a horse's hoofs. Men and their dealings, which I'd never understood, were left behind. Let me keep well clear of them and I might survive.

I noted the stars, so I should know if my road deviated from a northward line. (And I vowed that if I lived to do it I would mend two gaps in my education: I would learn to speak Russian and to read the stars. But I never did, of course.) I wondered whether Captain S was scanning that bright map above us. I must go warily. I was on a metalled road in a region strongly occupied by the Whites. Better get off the roads, where I risked meeting a patrol or coming on a guard post. So I did, without more trouble than the scratches inflicted by a hedge. The horse took the rougher going in its stride, though it lacked the style of my previous mounts.

The ground was pretty level. I avoided the dark masses of woodland. Later I might be glad of their shelter, but so long as I was wakeful I wanted to press into the night and win what ground I could, for I might be forced to hide by day. I thumped the horse's flanks, to impress this view on it.

Travel is a drug. The battle at the White headquarters had fallen into the silence to which I could consign all persons and events. The oblivious miles made all negligible. The only realities were my body on the horse's and the place I hadn't reached. Archangel glowed luridly in my imagination – a city of Byzantine grandeurs and great bells tolling and grey waters lapping deserted quays. It was well that the horse enjoyed going, as its kind do, for my thoughts were wandering. Still it knocked at the doors of heaven with its head – or seemed to, the ground being dark. Later the cloud thickened, snuffing the stars, and I had to rely on my remembrance of the terrain. The night was soundless except the beat of the hoofs that carried me.

Suddenly the darkness was broken by a red glare, irregular and indefinable, some distance ahead. It was accompanied by a noise equally mysterious. I stood aghast as a savage at this irruption into my dark and silent universe. It seemed at first to approach me slowly, and then to move rapidly in another direction. Aghast as I'd been at its approach, I was desolate at its withdrawal, as at the withdrawal of a special grace or revelation. I kicked my horse toward the glow, but the wonder receded more quickly than we could advance, and I found only cold railway lines as proof of its passing. For it had been a train.

Well, a train might be good or bad for me, depending on its passengers; but the exciting fact was that it had gone north. If I could buy or steal a ride on a northbound train I should save myself a lot of time. I'd heard of tramps in America travelling on the roofs of railway waggons – or even inside, snug under straw or tarpaulin. I followed the line back, to find the explanation of the train's change of direction. The track came from the west and branched here to go north and south, the choice being effected by an elaborate system of 'points'. Trains must pause here while the driver got down to alter the points. If I waited, hidden, near the track, I might be able to scramble aboard during that pause. It would be a case of scrambling, for nothing overhung the line. The nearest cover was a spinney some fifty yards away. I must wait there, and make a dash for it. There was no telling how long I should have to wait; but I might gain days by it, so a wait of hours was justified.

I settled us in that part of the spinney where we had the maximum of shelter compatible with a view of the line, and there we waited, shivering both from time to time but holding a tranced immobility. Of course the only trains running might be military, and I must think twice before jumping aboard one of those. I could only wait and hope. I hunched myself deeper in Grigor's coat, and marvelled that the cold air could still find entrance. But I was breathing deeply of the stuff, and any good I'd got from the Admiral's dinner had faded, leaving only nausea.

The night passed, the cloud occasionally parting to reveal the stars and then closing over them again. We were not the only dwellers there that night. I heard rustlings and utterances in the wood behind me, but only of birds and beasts harmless to me, whatever they were to each other. Dawn came, but still no train. Daylight reduced my chance of getting aboard unseen, and the sky showed no immediate likelihood of snow. The temperature was lower now than in the night – or long stillness had slowed my blood. I longed to gallop the horse to warm us both, but the western extent of the railway was hidden by forest, and I dared not risk being visible to a suddenly emerging train. The sky was like mother-of-pearl. A few birds wheeled in it, silently, also waiting. No town to be seen in the whole of the clear morning. Archangel might have been only a legend. I was growing impatient, though reason told me trains could be neither frequent nor regular. I began to say 'I'll wait so long and then go', as when somebody defaults on an appointment. But I'd no means of measuring time bar counting, and I always wearied of that before I reached the threatened number; so I stayed where I was.

Much later, when the sky had lost its pearl quality and was barred and blotched with a yellow which predicted storm, I heard, just beyond the western forest, the sound I awaited. Then, glancing at the junction of the tracks to judge the distance I must sprint, I noticed a lever beside the points and realised that the driver of a northbound train need alight to change the points only when he followed one which had gone south. Otherwise the points would be set in his favour and he would continue without pause – at speed, even.

I'd had all night to think of this, and several hours to see

141

it, and had remained blind until now when I heard the train approach! Should I change the points and risk being seen, or hope to leap aboard a speeding train? I wasn't confident of performing the latter trick, so I had no choice. The train's advance loud in my ears, though the thing itself was still out of sight, I raced my horse to the junction of the tracks, moved the lever, and raced back to cover. When I regained the spinney the engine had already appeared from the forest. I could only trust I'd been too quick for the driver's eyes, or that perhaps at that sleepy hour of the morning he saw no more than he expected to see. It was apparent that he'd expected to see the lever set in his favour, for the engine halted within a yard of it, I should say, with an abrupt restraint of power that sent a shudder back through the whole length of the train, which, to my great good fortune, consisted exclusively of goods waggons.

The driver got down and looked slowly round the landscape as if to spy out the joker who'd played this trick on him. I fancied he'd never seen that countryside before, though he might have crossed it every morning of his working life, and that he didn't know what to make of it. Then he looked up at the sky, as if he thought the hand of God had changed the points. Or perhaps he was only reading the weather. Then, a big spanner in one hand, he walked warily to the lever and moved it. As soon as his back was safely turned I tied my horse to a tree, sprinted to the train and climbed into the end waggon.

XI

The train moved again, and soon got up speed – as much to escape the scene of bafflement, I thought, as to regain lost time. So long as it went north it was taking me toward Archangel, and so soon as it deviated I could jump off, the ⌐iner by time and loser only by a horse, which I could replace. The horse didn't acquiesce in this view, and – I in my haste having tied it insecurely – galloped after the train to reproach me for my desertion. I don't know what the driver would have done if on top of his other supernatural experience he'd seen a horse chasing the train, but our speed soon took us beyond that danger.

I'd landed in a waggon half filled with coal – not the most comfortable of lounges. I knelt on it, I lay on it, I sat on it, I squatted on it. Each position had its peculiar pains. And rain water, or melted snow, had collected among the coals, so I was soon wet and daubed liberally with a kind of poor man's ink. The countryside continued flat, intermittently wooded, and deserted. Once or twice we stopped to take up water or coal, but always at a place where the apparatus for that operation was the only work of man. Of course each time it happened I was terrified that the driver had somehow learned of my presence, but that was impossible. The height of the intervening waggons and their loads effectively concealed me; there was no guard; and the stoker was so busy, poor devil, that he might as well have been down a mine for all the chance he had to look about him.

On we steamed, on through the infinite landscape and the eternal day. In Spain, they say, everything happens slowly because 'there's always tomorrow'. In Russia everything happened slowly because there was always today.

Still, our average speed was greater than a good horse's, and I took encouragement from the smoke which rolled massively overhead. I took not only encouragement, but a deal of soot on my clothes and person, so what with that and the coal dust I must have looked like a deported Negro before long. We kept going due north, and I began to have hopes we might be bound for the docks at Archangel. Mind you, I didn't know there were any docks at Archangel, but optimism isn't particular over niceties.

The day, which had never been bright, began to darken. I was hungry. It was no good getting a ride all the way if I arrived dead of starvation. But the crew must stop for food. Unless they carried it with them and ate with a free hand. The glare of the furnace was vivid in the dusk and I could see flame and sparks issuing from the tall smoke-stack. We seemed to increase speed after dark; but whether we did indeed, the crew perhaps fearing ambush, or whether it was an illusion caused by the disappearance of distant objects against which I had been able to measure our progress, I don't know. Anyway, darkness gave me a sense of hurry and excitement. But it didn't warm me or subdue my hunger. I must manage those two improvements soon, even at cost of leaving the train.

Some time after dark the glare of the furnace was augmented by other glares and lights and flashes ahead. At sight of them my hopes died. I knew these fireworks too well. There were the diagrams of death which only machine-guns can draw; there were the fiery belchings of field artillery; and there, in sequence of rank, the rifle flashes which look so weak against the others but can, well used and in sufficient number, vanquish them. The rifle fire fascinated me. It was an old familiar drill. Front rank fire and kneel to reload. Second rank fire and kneel to reload. And so on through as many ranks as you have; then the front rank stands to fire again. Or you can keep the front rank kneeling all the time, so that it and the second can fire together in a double volley. This formation and tactic – specially with the most capacious magazine, to the order 'Twelve rounds rapid!' – can make a good showing against all other kinds of fire. And there it all was. We had run into the middle of a battle.

Again a shudder ran backward through the train, hitting me with its collective force, as the driver applied the brake. He could retreat to safety, but then he would be late. He could go ahead, but then he would jeopardise his charge; for the combatants would see the train as a means of advantage and wouldn't be over-nice in commandeering it. Doubtful, the driver did what most of us do in doubt. He stood still. It was as unlucky as retreat or advance could have been. Instantly a mob of the losers – they'd lost heart even if they'd not yet lost the battle – swarmed onto the waggons, bearing their wounded; and a few minutes later the train proceeded, probably at the compulsion of pistol point.

My waggon, like every other, was crowded with refugees. They paid me no attention. They'd none to spare from their own distress. I've said they bore their wounded aboard; but I saw now that the wounded had pressed their company on the rest, who in some instances repulsed them with horror-stricken brutality, horrified that men could be so mutilated and live, that the obedient finger on the trigger could so disfigure what had been comely. Appalled, they pushed their wounded comrades from the waggons, hammered imploring fingers with the butts of rifles, frantic to repel those frightful reminders of the soldier's trade. Those things clawing at the walls of the waggons were like nothing on a recruiting poster. The less wounded who got aboard were bad enough to see – an ugly exposition of the beautiful flashes which continued on both sides of us.

Now the train was under fire. I couldn't make out whether we'd simply got between the combatants and were suffering the brunt of their exchange, or whether the victors were angry that any of their foe should escape. Whatever the

145

reason, the effect was the same. A hail of bullets struck the waggons, administering the coup-de-grace to some of the wounded and electing new casualties to fill the vacancies. We in our coal waggon were lucky. Its iron walls threw off many of the bullets. But it was overcrowded and several of its occupants rode unshielded. They struggled to oust their comrades from the safer places, and those others struggled to keep their places. Luckily, being first there, I lay beneath this contest; and I had no compunction in using any device to stay there. I didn't feel called on to be shot in a Russian civil war. No matter what I'd done in my own country, I had believed no Cyrillic recruiting poster nor submitted to any overlord's knout. I was neither Red nor White, but Red, White and Blue, I told myself, laughing hysterically, as I bit, twisted and kicked the hands that strove to dislodge me.

The train was putting on full steam. I guessed the driver and fireman needed no compulsion to do that. We had passed through the worst of the firing and were out into darkness and stillness again, the newly wounded, mostly in the wooden trucks, screaming like a trainload of damned souls at the gate of hell. And the stars shone just as before, and I was unhurt except a bruise and a scratch or two, and my image of Archangel was still vivid, though in those few minutes the images of many about me had been darkened for ever.

I was calm enough – for in that situation one chose between being calm and being crazed – to ponder my next movements. Proud as I'd once been of my masquerade as a wounded soldier, it would scarcely pass in a company of the genuine article. Not while I was wearing evening dress, at least. True a change of clothes was available. At least two of the men lying beside and on top of me had no further need of their uniforms; and the waggon was enough an anarchy of self-interest, a mixture of cage and hospital, for me to effect the change without being noticed. I shrank from the task, but the dead have a duty to the living and I must help

146

one of them discharge it.

Shivering with cold, shuddering at the touch of useless flesh, I pulled off my topcoat and tailcoat and trousers and drew on the coarse serge of a uniform that was wet with blood. One man saw what I was doing. It did not appear an act of sacrilege to him. He watched listlessly. Others only cursed my movement. I pulled Grigor's fur coat on over the uniform, and made sure that the coins were still in its pockets. The buttons had been wrenched from it and it was now smeared with blood on top of coal dust, but it might stand between me and death by exposure. Of course I now risked being shot as a deserter or ordered back to the fighting; but I didn't suppose the soldiers round me intended suffering either inconvenience, and if I went with them I might be safe.

I groped in the dark, among coals and ambiguous limbs, to find whether any of the dead or wounded had a revolver. But they had left their weapons on the field; and anyway sidearms were usually issued only to officers. These men wore the uniform of the old army, but they might be Reds who hadn't yet been re-clothed. It didn't matter to me so long as they went north and I could go among them.

The train went on, through eternal Russia, through eternal night. On under the stars with its irrelevant load. The talk of the soldiers dwindled into silence. Only the moaning of the wounded continued, over the senseless sing-song of the wheels. I sat watching the sky and the shapes of men against it. The blood on the uniform had dried. I was cold, and felt an intermittent nausea. But I was still alive, and still going the right way.

And then I slept, I suppose, for when I next looked at the sky its stars were extinguished, and the land on either side of the railway was widely built on. We were approaching a big town. It was not Archangel. We were descending to it, so I could see some way beyond it, and there was no sea. Only plain. The sun was rising. My companions were a gruesome sight. I don't know whether the living or the dead looked worse. At least the dead had a spurious dignity. The soldiers stared at me, but I was left alone. They had more pressing worries. A big town was no good to them either way. Being runaways, they had as much to fear from their own side as from the enemy. There was much excited talking and looking toward the engine. I wondered whether they had officers, or unofficial leaders, aboard. Many buildings in the town we approached had been damaged. The whole place had a charred appearance, and few people were about.

The train slowed and stopped in a station, that also blackened and damaged. Like an outing of schoolboys, all the soldiers who could run scrambled from the waggons, ran across the station, between sleeping tramps and vendors' stalls, and vanished into the town. I was left with the wounded. I was at a loss. My chosen escort had vanished, leaving me conspicuous. The driver and fireman of the train had vanished. Perhaps this was the terminus of their journey. The wounded lay in ungainly attitudes, like dolls broken and thrown away. I could do nothing for them. I walked across the station, accosted by creatures of indeterminate age and sex, bundled in rags, urging what plea or offering what service I could not tell. One of my gold coins would have concluded their business, no doubt, but those few coins might prove my stepping-stones to freedom. I could spare no more. Ashamed of leaving the wounded and refusing the supplicants, I hurried from the station.

The town was a desolate place. It had on it, and in its air, a cold greasy sweat of early morning. The streets were littered, and in places made nearly impassable, by rubble from the buildings which had been shelled, and were chiefly frequented by those homeless, masterless dogs characteristic of the Russian towns I saw. But men eat and drink even at the centre of calamity, and surely I should find breakfast if I searched long enough. I was walking up a steep narrow street. The low sun threw strange shadows and shafts of light down it toward me; and now among these motionless shadows of masonry I saw moving shadows – weirdly elongated but identifiable as those of men. Soon the owners appeared – themselves disappointingly small and ordinary. But their uniform seized my attention, being of the new Red army. A town patrolled by Reds was not a healthy place for me to wander in. The men came slowly down the street, swaggering in their little authority but obviously cold and irked by the rough serge of their uniforms. I knew all about rough serge. They were new recruits, I guessed, and were looking importantly about them with the bravado that comes of expecting to see nothing. They didn't seem to look specially at me. Unobtrusively, and not too hurriedly, I turned back. Only the trousers of my White uniform were visible; and those weren't necessarily incriminating at a time when half the Red Army was still wearing Tsarist uniform and when civilians wore anything they could lay hands on. But my fur coat, dirtied and bloodied, might excite question. So I turned back down the street, as slowly as I dared.

I had reached the bottom of it again, where it was intersected by several alleys, and was choosing which to take, when one of those confounded beggars from the station, whom I'd noticed because of his stooped height, drew near. Obviously he'd followed me, and it had taken him all this time to do it. Appalled by this encounter, which trapped me, and by his manic gaze, I didn't hear what he muttered. I turned desperately aside, but he laid a filthy mittened claw on my sleeve. The patrol was half-way down the street, seeming to hang poised above us in mid-air, their grandiose shadows still preceding them. 'Hey, Bud!' muttered the beggar as I tore my arm free. 'I'm on your side. Let's make it snappy.' He scuttled into an alley, with nods and beckonings and servile obeisances and a supplicating whine, all these done for the attention of the soldiers above us. I followed him. It sounded a native American voice; and anyway I'd no option. In the alley we stood to watch the soldiers pass. Then he drew from among the rags that wrapt him a piece of paper, a photograph. Had he brought me here only to sell me the kind of postcard that's touted in the East? But looking closer I saw he held a familiar poster, folded to show my portrait. 'I know who you are, you see,' he said. 'You don't need to know who I am. But you may care to know that an anti-Bolshevik government has been set up in Archangel with the support of our two countries. And, with your approval, we propose keeping you hidden here till we can get you under cover to Archangel, whence you'll be shipped home. Don't look so alarmed. You're not the first we've helped.'

'How did you know I was on that train?'

'I didn't. But we'd heard of your troubles down yonder – you're pretty well advertised, you see – and for days we've had somebody at every town on your route. As I guess the Ruskies ought to have, but they're a mite disorganised.'

Since he knew me, there was no more risk in believing him than in turning my back on him.

'Then I'm in your hands, Mr —?'

'Just Bud. That expression of confidence is mighty handsome of you on so short an acquaintance. I do assure you you won't live to regret it. Well, maybe that's not too happily phrased, but you get my meaning.'

He had the sprightliness of his race. It can sometimes appear the forced sprightliness of a man dancing on a tomb. His humour struck a morbid note in these surroundings, and he was too talkative for my liking; but both must be forgiven a man doing that job, which is lonely and anxious.

'What happens now?' I asked.

'Just follow me. Got any papers on you?'

'No. Only these,' I amended, remembering I'd felt the rustle of papers in the pocket of my stolen tunic, and now producing them.

'I'll hold on to these for the moment,' he said after a cur-

:ory glance. 'They could be useful later, but here you might is well wear this poster pinned to you. Just act dumb if anybody stops us. I'll do the talking. I guess I'll have to anyway. Is that right, you don't speak the language?'

'That's right.'

'It's a miracle you got this far.'

'At least I didn't hang myself with my tongue, as we say.'

'Meaning there's a danger I might?' He laughed.

'Is it safe to talk English so loudly here?' I looked up at the shuttered houses which overhung the narrow way.

'Safe enough, unless we run into a patrol. This is a city waiting for the gravediggers. It's been shelled by the Reds, it's been shelled by the Whites, and now it's waiting to see who'll have the next go. It doesn't listen to the living any more.'

We walked on. It was easy to believe his account. The few civilians we met shrunk out of our way like animals, with sidelong glances both malevolent and frightened, as if we might arrest them in their unlawful errand – which was usually that of looting, I suppose – and as if the sight of men walking erect and purposeful were an uncanny one. They were a dying people, expelled from their abode and nearly from life itself. Their hold on this their native town was failing. The shuttered houses drew back from them, awaiting new proprietors. We met no other patrol. Perhaps they avoided the back streets, as policemen avoided the London slums, fearing for their lives there. Our pace saved us, I believe; for the slowness of death was already on these creatures, so they were still revolving possible harms to us after we had passed them.

We reached a quarter which appeared to contradict my belief that all Russian towns ended abruptly, without suburbs. Beyond the last houses of the street we'd walked lay open ground, but in the middle of it stood another house. A house of some pretensions in its architecture, and seeming to demand more room than the others. But a second glance showed me that its solitude was of late occurrence It stood not in pleasant gardens but in the rubble of its recent neighbours. It alone had not been hit. 'Safest house in town,' laughed my guide. I laughed too, until I saw it was our destination. We walked to its front door like demure visitors, except that we had to kick aside the broken glass and bricks of other houses that could be visited no more.

'None of the citizens will come near it,' said the American. 'They think it's marked for the next hit. But I figure it's marked for preservation. I did hear it was the local whorehouse, and so neither side would shell it. But I doubt whether their gunnery's that good. Anyway, whoever lived here has decamped and the next bombardment isn't due for a day or two, so it seems just dandy for our purpose.'

'Is anybody else here?'

'I'm afraid not. You'll have only the ghosts of the girls to keep you warm.' He pushed the door open and led me in. The interior was prettily and expensively furnished, with a feminine touch.

'But I don't believe your tale,' I said. 'Obviously it was a private house.'

'I didn't say how many whores. Only one, maybe. High class. Generals only.'

There were French magazines, two or three years old. There was an open box of chocolates, some – the favourites – gone, leaving only their papers. There were dead flowers in a bowl. These signs of occupation troubled me, as if I stood in the scene of a supernatural abduction; though indeed there was nothing odd in anybody's leaving a house so imperilled. She had her life and looks to save. And if her reputation was true, she too may have doubted the aim, or even the goodwill, of her clients. I stood in her pretty house by as much right as anybody has to anything in war, but still I felt an intruder. The house was cold, and I shivered.

'There's firewood out back,' said the American. 'I guess you can get the stove going. I'll be back around nightfall. Don't open the door to anybody else – not that I think anybody else will come near. I dare say you'll know my voice.'

'I dare say I shall,' I said, not so much in mockery as because I found I could talk to him most easily by simply repeating one of his phrases.

'Otherwise we could agree a password – or a song, say.'

'Please let's not.'

So he skipped off without that precaution. I watched him go. As he entered the street we'd come by he assumed his crouched posture again. I think he was enjoying his work. Having bolted the door I went upstairs, because that was what I dreaded. I feared making an unpleasant discovery there, or suffering a further rebuke for my trespass; but any fact was preferable to the weight of those unknown rooms on my head. And of course there was nothing. Our worst fears are usually empty rooms. Only beds smoothly made on the last morning, and a little clock of gilt and enamel that had run down, and paintings of a mildly provocative kind, and a wardrobe full of rustling dresses that gave out a sad scent. Madame had left hurriedly and travelled light.

I went downstairs, my mind relieved of the upper storey, and with some trouble kindled a fire of damp wood in the stove, from which I had first to rake ashes. That done, there wasn't much else to do. I wound all the clocks and guessed a time to set them at. The larder was full of mouldy food, from which I salvaged a tin of biscuits, and from the cellar I got a bottle of wine; and thus provided I made an elegant bivouac, drawing a dainty sofa near the stove. But that again didn't kill much time, and I dared not drink enough of the wine to deaden sensibility, for I might still need my wits about me for all I was under the sprightly Yankee's protection. The trouble, as I speedily found, was that I wasn't much good at this kind of waiting war. All my escapades had been in the open and on the move. A few hours caged demoralised me; and my tolerance for the Yank's nervous traits, who spent his time waiting, grew.

I picked up and put down the few French books, they being of the same kind as the paintings. I've never found provocation an end in itself. I peeped from behind the curtains at the world outside. It was a world of broken bricks and steely sky. Moving streaks on the horizon might have been migrant birds or storm clouds distantly forming. The open end of the street gaped at me, a mouth about to utter a threat, but nobody came from it. The garden of Madame's house, where rubble and shattered glass were the only flowers, lay untrodden all day. The streaks on the horizon gathered and parted and passed, haphazard or deliberate according to their nature. I sat and stood again restlessly. I should have done better to sleep while I had the chance. I walked round the house, upstairs and down, looking from one window after another. No person appeared in any of the views. No sound of human activity, civil or military, reached me. I might have been marooned by the rest of mankind on this unlikely isle of a woman's elegance and silliness.

At dusk I drew the curtains and lit the several oil lamps, to cheer myself and to welcome the American. I wondered what he'd been doing all day; and of course I didn't fail to suspect he'd been selling me to the enemy, though reason told me the transaction would have been much sooner accomplished. Whatever he was doing kept him after dark. I ransacked the house for something useful, having despaired of finding anything amusing, but there was no map and no firearm. I wondered how reliable the Yankee's information on the date of the next bombardment was. At last, when I'd just fallen asleep in front of the stove, having exhausted all other occupations, the front door was rattled urgently, and on going to it I heard my new friend saying, 'It's me, Bud.'

154

'Madame's not at home,' I said. 'Come back another time.'

'Ha ha,' he said formally. 'You have a sense of humour, Bud. Now let me in. Time's life around these parts.'

So of course I let him in. There was nothing else to do. If was to get to Archangel I must let him in; but neither act seemed to me just then more desirable or easier than the other. He came in shivering, straight to the stove, where he stood warming his hands and glancing round. 'You certainly made yourself at home here,' he said.

'Of course. A glass of wine? A biscuit?'

'Both, please.'

'Has anybody you helped stayed here before?'

'Yes. I told you you're not the first.'

'What did they do with themselves?'

He looked up blankly from his wine, which he was quaffing while he still stood.

'I mean how did they pass the time?'

'I don't know. I didn't ask them. Why?'

'I just wondered.'

He looked at me thoughtfully and nodded. I'm afraid he thought me an odd character, not altogether worth saving. 'We're going to get you to Archangel by river,' he said firmly, as if a plain statement of the treatment might take our minds off my more distressing symptoms.

'By river?' I repeated, with a picture of swimming.

'Sure. Get you there on a barge. Safer than road. Relax. You're not the first.'

'Just remember some men like to think they are the first.'

'That's good. I thought you were one of those iced Limeys, but you sure have a sense of humour. I must remember that. "Some guys like to think they are the first." '

'Are you coming with me?'

'No. I've more to do here. There's quite a crowd of folk down yonder who'd like to get abroad for their health. But I'll tell you what to do. I'll draw you a map, in fact, and mark your way from the wharf where you'll be set ashore to the house where you'll wait. With luck you'll get there a night.'

'Surely there's no need of secrecy if the anti-Bolsheviks hold Archangel?'

'I guess you know your business better than I do, but the way I heard it the White boys were just as anxious to tall to you as the Red. The hostesses are just falling over each other to get hold of you, I heard. And although our two countries are supporting the set-up in Archangel they're not exactly running it. So maybe you'll do best to slip in and out without shouting your name.'

'You're right, of course. Sorry.'

'Here's the map. Just follow the dotted line. I've written the address. There's another invalid holing-up there, so you can bunk alongside him, and one of our people will be round to see you.'

'I think my own people will take care of me once I'm there.'

'Sure. We're working together. I know I don't look like somebody any government would trust, but wait till you see me in my own suit and I've had me a shave.'

He took me through the town again, through the same or a similar, tangle of back streets. There were more people in them now, moving in a shrouded, muted, furtive activity. I suppose the dark was better for their errands. On we went until we saw a strip of water catching the starlight and gleaming brighter than its surroundings. A barge loomed there, low and wide, its cargo sheeted with tarpaulin, and two horses harnessed to it, themselves darker than the darkness they were carved from; and on the quay stood its master, massive and featureless like his barge and beasts and nearly as silent. The whole business had a funerary look. Coins changed hands and the American helped me aboard.

'I don't know how to thank you,' I said.

'You don't have to. I'm on the payroll. See you after the war.'

Then the bargemaster shoved me down the companion-way with a hand in the small of my back, his other hand roughly ducking my head so it should miss the lintel; and the American and the stars vanished.

XII

The cabin I'd fallen into was small and dim and smelt of lamp oil. There were a cat and an old woman I believe. At least, so the sounds issuing from two formless bundles suggested, though the light was never good enough for me to verify the impression.

The barge proceeded smoothly and slowly, with a running ripple of the water it displaced and a jingle of harness. Before long the smell of oil began to make me feel sick. I would have gone on deck for air, but the master's firmness in pushing me below had indicated that I was to stay there; and I knew too well that I was a dangerous passenger, carrying whom he risked his liberty and life. He must want the payment badly. I wondered how long I was to stay below. I could foresee embarrassments, and I didn't suppose we'd any common language to resolve them.

Meantime the cat – if it was one – made noises of contentment or mild complaint on some system of its own; and the old woman – if she was – made an ancient crooning that might have been prayer or a recited knitting-pattern. I wondered whether my presence seemed as strange to them as theirs to me. Every appearance and circumstance of this journey by water and night seemed strange to me, but presumably for them it was commonplace to the point of boredom.

I tried to sleep, but I kept slipping nearly off the narrow bench that was fixed to the wall and knocking my head against the woodwork, and there were no cushions – not that I could find, at least. Presumably the bargemaster walked with the horses, or stood inscrutably on deck. Certainly he never came below.

Once a glass of tea materialised in my hand, probably put there by the woman; but I hadn't seen her make it and she said nothing to my thanks, so I wasn't sure even of that. I wondered how far Archangel was and how long we should take to reach it. The rest of our lives, at this speed. The American had spoken of my arriving there at night. It couldn't be this night. Tomorrow night? I wasn't sure I could bear more than twenty-four hours aboard the barge. I couldn't make my legs comfortable however I arranged them, and a tremendous draught, like an apprentice gale, came down the companion-way at me. The others didn't seem to mind it. Perhaps their wrappings made them proof against it, or perhaps I sheltered them, they sitting nearer the stove. In the end I devised a manner of sitting firm and dozed despite the draught.

Day had come when I woke. It showed the cabin less sinister than I'd imagined, but it scarcely made me wiser about my companions. The cat was nowhere to be seen. Possibly it materialised only in the hours of darkness. The other figure was rendered nearly cubic by its swathing of shawls. Shoes protruded at one end and a head at the other. But the head was sunk in sleep, face hidden, so that I saw only the kerchief tied round it. Two little hands, red and puffy and ringed, also protruded from the shawls and lay clasping each other for company in that desert of knitwear. The rings had been put on long ago, in a slimmer morning of romance, and were held immovable in ruts of the swollen flesh, not to be taken off this side the grave. The fire, like the cat, had gone out.

I looked on deck. The bargemaster was standing there, something of night clinging to the dark clothes he wore but all about him bright – even the horses, I saw with surprise. The barge itself was gaily painted with a device of flowers, and real flowers hung in pots everywhere a nail could be driven for that purpose. The master made no forbirring gesture at sight of me, so I supposed I was free to

159

come on deck. Which I did and stood beside him. He turned his head a fraction toward me and turned up the corner of his mouth and grunted, which in him constituted an exuberant greeting probably. The country we were passing through was empty enough for my presence on deck to be harmless and flat enough for us to spy danger a long way off. I was glad to stretch my legs and breathe the air.

The sun hadn't long been risen, and a whirl of colours remained about it that would evaporate soon. We had travelled farther than I'd supposed. I could see nothing of the town we'd left. We floated in an infinity of marshland, drawn on as in a dream by the somnambulist horses. Frogs croaked and birds rose noisily from the reeds at our approach and flew away low over the water.

I wondered what provisions we carried for breakfast. Since we'd enjoyed the luxury of tea in the night I reckoned I could look forward to a decent meal. And so it proved. Comprising cold fowl and pickled cabbage fiercely seasoned, it wasn't just the meal I would have chosen, but I felt better for it; and the coffee was perfect, being so hot it scalded my throat. I felt kindly toward everybody. The bargemaster was a fine fellow. His wife – or was she his mother? – was everything a woman should be. The cat was the best of its species.

I was happy to be with ordinary people again, and even found a pleasure in our slow rate of advance. I sat crosslegged on deck beside the man, watching him do something mysterious with a coil of rope. He puffed his pipe, and occasionally jerked his thumb or extended a forefinger at what he thought would interest me, and the day took its rhythm from these slow avocations.

Despite the soporific influences I did sometimes strain my eyes to see whether the desired city had yet risen from the dream terrain to print itself on the sky, but it never had. We had strayed far from the ways of men. We saw no traveller nor passed any boat. Only the birds that rose and fell, calling harshly and beating their wings in derisory applause. It was a paradise for sportsmen, but they had found other marks and the wildfowl flourished.

This day-long calm was pleasant after many turmoils, but it was incredible too, and a mite uncanny, as the Yankee would say, when darkness laid its lines about us again. The meres that lay on both sides of the river, draining or swelling its current, reflected the sky and the last of the light there so faithfully that I could hardly distinguish sky from water at any distance. And still the calm rested on everything, so profound that I felt it could not endure and caught myself holding my breath, listening for the sound that must break it. I watched the horses – massive against the sky as seen from my low view-point, for latterly I had been lying on the deck, my head against the cabin and my hands behind my head for a pillow. On they plodded, as if they would never falter in an enterprise no matter how foolish they thought it. It seemed a strange occupation for the man and woman too, this slow passage through country they never looked at.

The country was changing about us as daylight faded. The marshes were drying out, so to speak, and the horizon on either hand was rising into crags. It's not an hour to be sure of anything you see, but I was sure enough of the mounted sentry or look-out man on one of those crags to point him out to the bargemaster. We stood staring a moment, trying to pierce the fast gathering veils of darkness and mist. Then my companion motioned me to go below. If we could see the sentry, he could see us, even without the field-glasses he probably carried; and while there was no special reason for him to investigate a passing barge, he might fancy the ride.

In the cabin I strained my hearing, but could catch only the incessant caress of wood and water. Shortly afterwards the bargemaster came below – an act unprecedented in my experience, and therefore ominous – and spoke to the woman. It was the first time I'd seen them together. In going out he enjoined me to keep quiet, with a finger on his mouth

– not that I needed bidding – and gestured toward the shore. When he'd gone I was conscious of a subdued commotion in the cabin and of an unusual panting and breathlessness in the old woman's monologue, and I saw by the light of the stove that she was divesting herself, with difficulty, of her clothes. This seemed scarcely the moment to make her toilet, and I was in two minds whether I should withdraw discreetly, despite the danger outside. I was still pondering this point of etiquette when she took hold of me and began to wrap the discarded shawls round me. To be made a kind of cocoon by somebody I'd not been introduced to was grossly improper. I protested, but she only put another shawl over my head and pushed me into the seat opposite hers, evicting the cat. Now I saw her purpose, and I had to admit it was a pretty effective disguise in that dim cabin. But I didn't much like it. I'd sunk even lower than 'hiding behind a woman's petticoats'. However, there was nothing better to do, and already a drumming of hoofs was audible, followed a minute later by a challenging cry.

The barge stopped – but not too soon, the master obviously feeling his authority as good as a common soldier's – and I heard the newcomer clambering on board. I groped on the floor for any fire-iron that might serve as a weapon, but could find none. A conversation was heard overhead. The soldier did most of it, the bargemaster answering in surly monosyllables. Then boots clattered on the companion-way, an oath told us that the intruder hadn't ducked in time, the door was flung open and his figure bulked against the sky, a bright star visible over his shoulder like an epaulette.

He spoke, and the old woman answered. I sensed rather than saw that although addressing her he was looking at me. I could only trust she was telling him a good story. Luckily he'd no torch. He came nearer and touched me on the shoulder. He'd only to pull away the shawl that hid my beard and our little comedy would be ended. In a cracked falsetto I hummed one of the folk-tunes I'd heard in my

162

travels. Perhaps I'd heard it at the girl's house, where there were the crumbled coat-of-arms and the bird in a cage that I should never see again. Perhaps at Grigor's, when the peasants came to entertain us. I was so frightened that I forgot the soldier's presence and escaped into those other times, losing myself in the song that rises and falls in waves of passion and grief; but the passion grows weaker and the grief stronger, as if the singer aged, and all fades away in yearning; and latterly I was aware that the soldier was singing with me and I stopped and let him finish it alone; and then he was self-conscious and grinned and said farewell and climbed toward the stars, treading on the cat, which howled dismally; and we heard him ride away.

I thanked the old woman, hoping my tones would convey my gratitude, and made to return the shawls, but she put me firmly back into my seat. She had her wits about her, that one. The barge resumed its dreamy progress; the wood and water caressed in passing again and the harness on the horses jingled. But soon afterwards the noise of several horses grew through and over these sounds, and a great coldness replaced my little warmth of relief. Either the soldier hadn't been deceived and had simply gone for help, or his superiors didn't trust his judgment and had come to see for themselves.

I hurried on deck. The bargemaster stood stolidly at his post – because he was imperturbable or because he relied on the woman. I peered desperately all ways in the dark. I was trapped. Whichever way I ran I should be overtaken. And hiding was no good. They knew three were on board. I was aware of the woman behind me. Without ceremony she took hold of me and the bargemaster – one in each hand, it seemed – and drew us below. She didn't need to pull hard: we followed at a touch, stumbling but unprotesting, drawn by the prestige of the one who remains resolute. In the cabin she exchanged my shawls for the man's coat and cap. His sleeves ended high above my wrists, but it didn't matter in the dark. Meantime he at her bidding wrapped himself in the shawls. Then she pushed me on deck and him into my corner. She was a master-mind, fitter for my work than I was.

The next few minutes happened exactly as she had foreseen. I took up the man's station on deck. The horsemen – five or six of them – jumped on board and hurried below without a glance at me. They knew all about me. A most tremendous row ensued in the cabin, and a sound of one object being struck several times – or several similar objects struck in succession – against the wall. He was a stalwart fellow, that bargemaster, and I shouldn't have liked to get on the wrong side of him. I didn't loiter. Immediately the soldiers were below I vaulted from the deck into the saddle of the nearest of their horses, striking at the others with a length of wood I'd seized from the deck, and away the lot of us sped, the riderless horses soon streaking off back the way they'd come and I holding mine along the tow-path.

I heard cries behind me. The soldiers had discovered their mistake; but it would take them a long time to rectify it. Providing the couple on the barge weren't hurt, I didn't mind. The worst of it was that the Reds now knew my position. But if I could keep going that didn't matter too much, for I must be nearing Archangel and would soon be out of their territory.

It was good to be riding again. The path was easy and the horse obedient, so I'd little to do. The river gleamed or glittered on my right, according to its speed and currents. I should reach the appointed wharf simply by following the river. Presumably the horses drew the barge all the way, and where they could go my new mount could. I checked that I still had the Yankee's map in my tunic pocket. The crags on the eastern and western skylines drew closer and were gradually subdued. The skyline ahead I couldn't make out. It was confused and variously massive.

The river banks were succeeded by embankments of masonry and the tow-path became more definite. I reckoned

I was approaching a town, and I had a sense, though I suppressed it incredulously, that it was Archangel. Scattered lights were now visible among the irregular masses in the north. I longed for a moon to show me more. I had almost a dread of attaining what had been so long desired. A big town, the biggest I'd yet seen, was every minute declaring itself more unmistakably ahead. I saw more and more lights, which had been hidden by trees rather than precaution, and could even make out the shapes of buildings. If this was Archangel – and I could no longer subdue the belief that it was – I need fear no more pursuit.

In the interest of a modest arrival, as advised by the Yankee, I might do well to leave the horse here and go the rest of the way on foot. The rest of the way! It was incredible that only a mile or two remained of the journey that had often seemed hopeless. I was almost wistful for the miles that lay behind, now I was assured of arrival. I dismounted and slapped the horse encouragingly, but it followed me, so I tethered it to an iron ring that was fixed in the wall beside the path.

I walked on alone, small and humbled in the starry night, conscious of not deserving my good fortune, or anyway of deserving it no more than others who lay dead or prisoner. I had arrived. I was within sight of safety, even though perils stood between. If I should survive I must make good use of my life. It's not a moment to dwell on. It's not necessary to the story, and the discrepancy between intent and act is too reproachful.

I walked along the tow-path, the city growing tall on both banks of the river, and the river itself, which had long been the chief feature of the landscape, suddenly insignificant – a mere rumour of open country, a mere reflection of the city's lamps, no longer taking precedence but diverted to run ignominiously among back streets and behind warehouses. Nonetheless, like me, it was nearing its goal.

I found myself now at the wharves, where many barges

were loading and unloading under the light of naphthalene lamps. Sentries patrolled the wharves, but there was no apparent check on people entering the town and I went unchallenged. The Red armies would not put their noses into a shop where Britain and America sat in the back room. I took the Yank's map from my pocket and compared it with what I saw. They corresponded exactly. In one or two instances he'd sketched the elevation of a building, and these little pictures confirmed my position. I was in Archangel. I sat on a mooring-post and wept. Nobody gave me a second glance. There was plenty to weep about in Russia then – specially for a man in uniform, who might return to find his family dead – and they didn't know I wept for joy.

When I'd recovered I looked at the map again and followed the dotted line. It led me away from the wharves, between churches and into a prosperous residential quarter. So far the city wasn't at all as I'd imagined it. I found the appointed house without difficulty. It was quite a mansion, the kind of merchant's house you find in old sea-ports all over the world, built with the profits of trade, founded firmly on the stooped backs of slaves, and stationed half-way between the urban society the merchant would impress and the port where his business lay. It stood tall and had a 'don't-come-in-unless-you're-very-rich' look. Most of the windows were shuttered. That was common in Russia. I never determined whether it was done against the cold or the people; but certainly most houses had shutters, some both inner and outer. I lifted the heavy brass knocker – it was stiff on its hinges – and gave a knock that echoed up and down the cobbled street but had no other apparent effect. I stepped back into the street and stared up at the house to detect any sign of life. Then I looked for a bell, but there was none. I tried the reluctant knocker again.

The door was opened by the most scared-looking little girl I'd ever seen. I suppose she was in her mid teens, but, enveloped in an apron too big for her and with hair disordered, she might have been a few years either side of that. I showed her the Yankee's map, thinking it my best credential. She nodded impatiently and beckoned me in, looking nervously behind me as if the massed Bolsheviks might be in the street. Immediately I stood inside she bolted the door. Presumably she was a maid-servant of some kind, but I didn't think she'd last long in the job if it worried her this much. The rescue organisation had strangely assorted members, judging by my too bright American and this terrified girl. Signifying that she didn't understand English, she took my coat, in purely mechanical recollection of a calmer time when such things were done, and pointed up the stairs, herself scurrying into the basement. I walked slowly upstairs, smiling at this odd reception, and opened the double doors at the head of the stairs.

XIII

Captain S stood just inside. Apparently he had been about to open the doors. I can't swear that he jumped backward the length of the corridor, but certainly one minute he stood facing me, scarcely a foot between us, and next he was at the far end of the corridor, still facing me, his face perceptibly paler and his hands groping the blank wall behind as if it might somehow save him. I knew from this action that he was unarmed. Otherwise my story must have ended there, untold. In the first instant of seeing him I'd supposed the American had played me false, sent me into a trap; but in that case the Captain would have been better prepared. He must be the other 'invalid' who was waiting here to be got abroad. The Whites were after him for desertion and the Reds for neglect of duty. Either he hadn't been told of my coming or hadn't identified me from the description. I supposed he'd heard my knocking and had come to see the cause. He looked as if he'd been going to bed, for he wore a dressing-gown over plain trousers.

'I won't hurt you,' I said. I said it to break the weird silence that held us apart yet locked us together, and to remove that stricken look from his face. I thought for a moment he'd lost his wits under the shock of my appearing. I must restore him to something more resembling humanity. He shook his head slowly. It wasn't at all a reply to my words, but done as if he were trying to dispel an hallucination. Failing in that, he seized the handle of the door nearest him – there were several on both sides of the corridor – and tugged it violently, never taking his eyes off me. But either the door was locked or in his fright he was pulling it the wrong way. It stayed shut, and after a few minutes he left off his attempt and stood panting.

I had closed the double doors behind me, so that we stood in what was in effect a long, low, narrow wooden box. Like a coffin. As I've said, there were several other doors, and presumably one of them must be unlocked; but to reach them he must come nearer me, and that seemed a thing of which he was physically, let alone mentally, incapable – even if he remembered which door he'd come through. There was a window behind him, sunk in the thickness of the wall, and now, still without taking his eyes off me, he pulled himself up to its ledge and tried to open it, apparently ignorant that it was not made to open and was barred too. I'd said nothing after my first remark. He stood in the window recess, glaring down at me. I don't know what I would have done if I'd been armed. Just what I did, probably. I know what he would have done had he been armed. He was indisputably the better realist. Except at this unfortunate juncture.

I said 'What are you doing here?' I spoke gently, as if I had to wake a sleep-walker. He did then relax enough to look away from me for a minute. He looked up at the ceiling. A lamp hung there, and I wondered whether he was reckoning his chance of smashing it. Anyway it was out of reach. He lowered himself to sit on the window ledge, legs dangling, and said, 'You made things difficult for me. I have to get away. I should not have expected you to lie. I thought you a gentleman.' The effrontery of this left me without answer, and he sat swinging his legs, like a child caught in a misdemeanour who manages to transfer the blame. 'It's time for a truce,' he said. 'We have to live together here until they get us away, so we'd better live peaceably.'

'I don't trust you,' I said. 'I know that if you get hold of a gun first you'll use it.'

We had both spoken abnormally slowly, as if engraving our words. He slid down from the window ledge, shrugging, with something of his old feline grace, and opened one of the doors easily, without hesitation, and passed from the corridor without looking back. I followed close. He might have a gun somewhere. I kept at his heels right into his room.

'Where are my quarters?' I said.

'I really can't say. There are rooms ready all over the house.'

'Can't you ask the maid?'

'I can, of course, but she's a little affected in her wits, poor soul.'

She might easily be, I thought; but all the same I wasn't convinced of it. He habitually told lies, not with any particular object but as a man might set snares at random – hoping to get some advantage from them later.

'Then I shall take the room next yours,' I said, pushing open a communicating door. 'And I'll make sure you've no weapon hidden here,' I said, searching first his few clothes that hung in a wardrobe and then the dressing-table and chest-of-drawers and even the bed.

'This is not polite behaviour,' he said.

There was no weapon.

'Are there servants here beside the maid?'

'Not to my knowledge.'

Again I thought he was lying. I must find out for myself. I went downstairs and locked the front door and pocketed the key. Then I knocked at the door through which the girl had gone, and in a moment she appeared, looking scarcely less frightened than before. I smiled in an attempt to put her at ease; but I was a grim figure, unwashed, uncombed, clothes blood-stained and black with coal, and probably a smile only aggravated the effect. I put her gently aside and went down the farther flight of stairs to investigate. I found a great bare kitchen, stone flagged, lit by candles. There were no other servants, but men's boots and a coat hanging on a door showed that at least there had been.

I went upstairs again and inspected the room I'd chosen. It was palatial compared with my recent lodgings. The

Yankee had a talent for finding grand houses untenanted. Perhaps it wasn't difficult just then. I was pleased to see that the communicating door had bolts on my side as well as on the Captain's. Very civilised – only by consent of both parties. The Captain was standing where I'd left him. I think he was still suffering shock. 'Do we get any supper?' I said.

'I'll ring for some. I've had mine.'

So presumably the girl had wits enough for that. I shut the door and pushed home the bolts. I heard the maid answer his bell and go away again, and after a long delay she brought me a tray of food. There was nothing hot, but there was an unopened half-bottle of wine. When she'd gone I found matches on the mantelpiece and set light to the pre-pared fire, which surprised me by blazing immediately. It didn't warm that Arctic room much, but it made it more cheerful. I sat in bed, wearing my uniform still, and ate my supper luxuriously. Then I slept, without time even to take off my tunic or extinguish the lamps.

I woke at daylight smiling from happy dreams. Sunlight filled the room, flooding in through unshuttered windows and penetrating the fine curtains so that their pattern of flowers and butterflies appeared to grow and dance in sun-light. Not even the presence of my enemy next door could mar my pleasure in the new day and in life resumed. Beyond the window was sunlight, and beyond that sea, and beyond that England, where the crocuses were in flower. I drew the curtains and stood letting the sun warm my face. It must have been the sabbath, for bells were tolling as they had done in my dream of the city. But nothing else was as I'd imagined it. The houses I saw were cleaner, brighter, and the street was far from being unpeopled.

I found a ewer of hot water at my door, and having made the best toilet I could I went downstairs, hearing voices there. Captain S was talking to the girl in a big room where the table had been laid for our breakfast. Dust sheets were still over much of the furniture, so that our two uncovered chairs had an appearance of standing among ghosts. The conversation was broken off as I entered. The girl seemed to curtsey to me, but since she seemed continually to duck from expected blows or imagined dangers it was hard to tell. I smiled again.

'I trust you slept well,' said the Captain; and we took our places.

'Excellently,' I said; and the girl made tea.

'It's a pity we meet again in difficult circumstances,' he said when she'd gone. 'I had looked forward to continuing our literary discussions. You were guilty of an ungentlemanly act in defaming me. The fools believed you – or affected to – and in consequence my photograph is advertised everywhere with yours and I'm obliged to fly my own country.'

I found that funny. But I didn't laugh outright. He appeared sincerely distressed. Also he appeared to be pursuing his grievance with a morbid intensity that might burst into fury at any minute. I reckoned his recent experiences had thrown him off balance – off as much balance as a man choosing that profession can have had in the first place, that is.

'I don't know what I shall do abroad,' he said.

'You'll do better than you would here. The Reds would never trust a turncoat.'

'The Red army is recruited from turncoats.'

'My point stands. You speak English well. You'll prosper in America.'

'Why not in England?'

'You speak it too well for England.' I didn't add, Because I'm going there. He was a cancer that must be cut out of my life. He said no more, but I could see he hadn't let go of his grievance. I hoped the American's local representative would call soon. After breakfast S sat with a newspaper in front of his face – it was the official publication of the new

172

Archangel government, he told me – but I'd an uncomfortable suspicion that he was using it merely as a cover from behind which he could study me.

'You must have been surprised to find Archangel in White hands,' I said.

'Yes. Fortunately the poster denouncing me was a recommendation to our American friend. You did me a good turn there.' He raised the paper again.

I walked round the house. I should have liked to go out. It was hard to believe there could be danger in those sunny streets, among those decent people. The house had no garden. Perhaps they weren't the fashion there; or perhaps the merchant hadn't spent money on what didn't impress people in the street. I sat at my window and looked longingly out, like a love-sick girl. I had opened the window, and snatches of talk came to me, and the scent of flowers from window boxes, and the smoke of cigarettes. These were the first evidences of ordinary life I'd had in a long time. Other towns I'd seen, nearer the fighting, exhausted by conscription and requisition if not actually damaged, had lived under stresses that forbade gentle occupations. Archangel had been lucky. I scanned the people, trying to find an American appearance among them. But there was no reason the local man should be American, and even if he was he might, like his compatriot, affect bizarre disguise. Anyway, nobody turned aside to the house where I sat, nor even glanced at it. Obviously its history was as uninteresting to them as its present use.

The day passed, the shadows changing angle and lengthening. The church-going traffic was succeeded by a noon lull and that by the afternoon promenade and that by another procession of worshippers. Then darkness held the street again, and stars the sky. Captain S knocked at my door.

'Shall we try to resume our good relations?' he said.

'Resume?'

'Two men of taste and intelligence ought to be able to

converse despite the accidents of war.'

'Somebody else said that to me. He was German.'

'Let us go downstairs, and have lamps lit and wine brought, and talk of books and the lasting things.'

I couldn't spend all night sitting at the window. And anyway I'd rather have him where I could see him. 'Very well,' I said.

Downstairs he rang for the fire to be lit in the icy drawing-room. The same girl served us, her dress and manner unchanged. I wondered how she spent her time. Looking after us didn't demand much of it. She brought bottles of wine and glasses and left us to our convivial evening. Captain S hadn't read any more English authors since our last discussion of them, nor had he developed any new thoughts on the old ones, but he resumed favourite questions, appearing to solicit my opinion respectfully. I wondered what he really wanted. I was careful to drink less than I appeared to.

Late in the evening, when wine and talk had run down to their dregs and we sat staring at the fire, we were startled by a knocking at the street door. The house where we sat comfortable was instantly transformed to a trap where we sat defenceless. I don't know whether I took fright from the Captain's face or he from mine. 'Let the girl answer it,' he said. But she didn't and the knocking, scarcely left off, was repeated. We looked at each other and rose and went together to the door, which trembled under the caller's urgency. Captain S challenged in Russian and received an answer satisfactory enough to induce him to draw the bolts. He still couldn't open the door without its key, which I took from my pocket. He looked at it but said nothing, and I completed the opening.

A decently dressed man, who might have been one of the church-goers I'd seen, walked in smiling and shut the door again. He spoke to the Captain in Russian and then to us both in English. 'I am a friend of Bud's,' he said. 'I am sorry I could not come to see you sooner, but you will understand that we are busy and that our business is not easy.' We went to the drawing-room. 'Ah,' he said at sight of the empty bottles, ' "Drink deep, think deep," we say.' I didn't believe they said it. I suspected he'd invented it that minute, in mere courtesy to me. The Russians are like that. He paused, as if to see whether we would propose having another bottle up. 'Now,' he said. 'We have hopes of getting you, sir, aboard a British ship without delay. News of your arrival has been passed to the British authorities here' – so the girl did something beside her household tasks – 'and they intend to pick you up tomorrow night. They may be willing to take you too, Captain. That's all for the moment, and I must be off. You're being well looked after?' Of course we assured him we were, and away he went. He was a reserved man, for all his show of affability. Probably he needed to be.

I thought Captain S had been worried by the visit. Maybe it was the doubt about his being got away. Anyway, our convivial evening ended then. The fire was dead, the wine finished, the girl not to be roused to fetch more, and our interest in literature, such as it was, exhausted. On my way to bed I locked the house door again, keeping the key. I locked my own door, too, checked that the communicating door was still bolted, fastened the shutters – for the night was cold, and the room chill from long disuse – and undressed. It's amazing how quickly a strange room becomes home, how quickly the mind puts out roots. With the prospect of soon leaving it I felt quite wistful for this room where I had begun to arrange my few possessions – putting Grigor's gold coins in piles of different denominations on the dressing-table, for instance. I lay in bed remembering home and the possessions I'd left there. I suspected I had outgrown both the possessions and the promises. Then I slept. The Captain's light was still on.

I slept badly. I couldn't make out whether the house had rats, but there was a scuffling and scurrying at intervals, not loud enough to investigate but loud enough to disturb me;

and when I did sleep I dreamed unpleasantly. I was glad when morning came, though morning brought its problems. I must decide today what to do about Captain S. Easy to say Do nothing, but be on your guard. In fact to do nothing was tacitly to vouch for him and assist his escape abroad. I wondered why he had lied about the girl and the absence of other servants – I was sure he had – and wished I'd asked our visitor.

The Captain was already at table when I went down. He had taken my place, facing the door. 'I trust you don't mind,' he said. 'I wanted to be nearer the stove. I fear I took a chill sitting up too late last night.' I murmured that he was welcome and took the chair opposite him. 'So this may be our last day together,' he said. 'If your people refuse me a passage. Or if you denounce me to them, for which I couldn't altogether blame you.' He looked at me quizzically, and then chattered on. He was unusually talkative and I didn't listen much. I heard the girl come in to clear the plates, and heard S saying, 'But I must make one more attempt to redeem myself in the eyes of my superiors.' And how d'you suppose you'll do that? I wondered. Then I saw that more than one person had come into the room, and that they had not come to clear the table. Three men stood with the girl, all looking toward the Captain.

'As one who has himself been forced into falsehood,' he said, '– for I cannot believe you lied about me except under absolute necessity – you will forgive me a little lie in my turn. As you see, and as you probably suspected, the house does indeed have more than one servant. And apparently my prestige as an officer of the secret police still sways them. At least enough to enlist their help in my last attempt.'

He addressed the servants in Russian. The girl and the eldest man then did clear the table, the other two guarding the door. There was no good in starting a fight. One of them had a revolver. The cleared table was pushed against the sideboard where the samovar stood. I was seized and laid on the table face upward, wrists and ankles lashed one to each of its legs. My face was immediately beneath the tap of the samovar, and I could guess the nature of the Captain's last attempt even before somebody's fingers were knotted in my hair to hold my head still. Carefully, like a doctor, Captain S secured my eyelids with adhesive tape so I couldn't blink.

'I know that pain is nothing to you,' he said. 'But think of the irreparable damage. Think of the faces in England you will never see again. You can save your sight and my credit by telling me what your mission here was. I will smoke a cigarette while we wait for the water to boil.'

In choosing to be blinded rather than confess, I wasn't brave. It seemed to me – it had been drummed into me, I suppose, by the whole training of my childhood, long before my training as a spy – that there was really no choice. Boys' books were full of heroes enduring agony and death rather than betray their country. I saw no practical good in my silence. What did it matter, now exhausted Russia had begged Germany for peace, that I had been sent to judge whether she might change sides? What did it matter if her demoralised armies did obey the Kaiser, come to that? They'd be no more help to him, I reckoned, than they had been to us. But silence was my duty. I only wished the scene of it had been more like those in the stories, instead of this ceiling of moulded plaster and the Captain's scented face.

When he had finished his cigarette he tested the water in the samovar and judged it ready. 'By a nice adjustment of the tap,' he explained, 'I can cause it to drip. A stream of water would be crude. You know me. You know I like to proceed by degrees.'

I saw the drop of water forming at the mouth of the spout. Forming, swelling. Beautiful it was, and monstrous. Forming and swelling through a lifetime. I saw it fall. I swear I saw it fall. I felt it sear the eyeball. I lost consciousness.

'My dear chap,' said Captain S when I was revived, 'you don't do yourself justice. You've overtaxed yourself. Your nerve is gone. And that was only cold water. Feel.' He untied my hand and put it under the tap. He spoke truth. 'What will you do when it's really boiling?'

I didn't know what I should do. I could no longer answer for myself. I'd withstood his persuasions at the fortress but I had not forgotten them, and the accumulated weight of remembered pain and despair might at last bear down the flood-wall. I had endured so much only to fall into his hands again, as if fate had assisted him in designing a prolonged torture worse than all the others. But at least I remained silent under his taunt. I had learned, at some cost, that silence annoyed Captain S.

'Now I am in earnest,' he said. 'We have played for a moment, but time runs short. I shall smoke another cigarette, until the water is boiling indeed.'

He was suffering not scruples but qualms, I thought. If he were to blind me in vain – if I were still to keep silent – he would have forfeited his chance of getting abroad and would have nothing to placate his masters. He sat on the end of the table, between my tied feet, watching me. The servants stood looking on, as the Russian people had looked on at so many extraordinary occurrences. They were, as ever, the unknown quantity in the situation – strong enough to reverse it if they chose, being three to one even excluding the girl and having a gun besides, but probably cowed by their long remembrance of the secret police. Like me, they were frightened of the past. An accumulation of fear, rather than any present danger, would prevent their intervening, just as it might force me to confess. And anyway, even had they been well disposed toward me, I'd no means of asking their help. I couldn't talk to them. I couldn't even catch their eyes. Perhaps deliberately, they averted them, keeping their gaze on the Captain. Except the girl, whose eyes once met mine. I smiled, but she only frowned and looked away.

178

'Now we are ready,' said the Captain. 'Feel, so you don't entertain unfounded hopes of a second reprieve.' He put my hand to the tap. The water was boiling. My hand was tied again. 'Please prepare yourself,' said Captain S.

Someone else spoke. Another voice was so unexpected that I couldn't understand what it was at first. But the girl had spoken. And whatever she had said had arrested the Captain's hand. The other fingers released my hair and I raised my head to see what was happening. The girl had got the gun. She might be out of her wits – if not, she was lion brave – but she had got the gun. Not expecting attack from that quarter, the man who'd held it must have relaxed his grip, and she had acted with that swiftness of action swifter than any man's which some women sometimes command. Obviously her word, or the gun, carried more weight than the Captain's erstwhile prestige, and he had lost control of the situation. This change took no more than an instant, and I was still watching the two chief actors in it, wondering what they would do next, when the house resounded to a knocking at the front door. Captain S took advantage of this diversion to escape from the room, nobody preventing him despite my cries. I heard him answer the door, and a moment later our visitor of the previous night appeared, alone. To whom the girl spoke.

'This is most distressing,' he said on seeing my plight. I thought it an understatement. The menservants untied me, the newcomer and the girl talking Russian all the time. 'I am so very sorry that this has happened,' he said. 'We spare no effort to ascertain the good faith of our clients.'

'Did he get away?'

'I left him ostensibly shutting the door. Of course I did not know what had happened. I came to tell you that the British warship will come in earlier than we expected – at three this afternoon.'

'Why did the girl help me?'

'Fortunately she speaks English. The Captain was not

aware of her accomplishment.'

'Nor was I.'

'Quite. We do exercise some degree of supervision over our guests, you see. She was not privy to the Captain's intention – though I fear these fellows were – and had to act very quickly.'

I thanked her as best I could. She accepted my thanks frowning, as probably she would accept everything that came to her. She was the last of the Russian women who helped me, for no advantage to themselves, and stands in my remembrance representative of that kindly, incalculable race.

'I must find him,' I said, and took the revolver from her. She relinquished it willingly, almost disdainfully, now it had served its purpose. In her eyes it was once more a plaything for children. I wondered whether she could have fired it.

'But the streets are dangerous,' said the little man. 'Your picture's everywhere.'

'His picture's everywhere too, so we start even.'

In the hall the girl helped me into my coat, the man trying both verbally and physically to restrain me.

XIV

A sleety rain was falling, like needles flung in your face, and the streets were empty. I couldn't tell which way S had gone, but I didn't pause to speculate. We were fated to meet. He had forfeited his chance of escape. He would be desperate and ferocious, like a cornered beast.

The sky was overcast. Leaden clouds seemed to rest on the roofs and chimneys. The sleet was whitening, hardening into hail. With my left hand I turned up the collar of the bargee's coat. My right hand I kept on the butt of the revolver. I was conscious that the little Russian had followed me, but my quick stride held him at a distance. He had no part in the affair. He could be only a spectator. Captain S and I were alone concerned. Only we two in the emptied and whitening streets, as only we had been in the cells of the fortress and in the night ride from Grigor's. Only we were in Russia, his assaults on my integrity determining the character and pace of my whole experience there.

I passed two or three other pedestrians whose business compelled them to walk the worsening storm, but they were too occupied in huddling into their coats and keeping their hats on to spare me more than one glance. I had emerged from the street of merchants' houses and had crossed a square when I heard my name called behind me. I took cover in a doorway and peered back across the square. Nobody in sight. Because of the thickening snowfall I couldn't see far. Echoes had distorted the voice beyond recognition. Possibly the little Russian had called to warn me of danger. Possibly Captain S had called and was waiting for me to answer and so to betray my position. He might have got a gun somehow. Or possibly I'd dreamed the voice. Possibly it had been the cry of someone not in Russia – not alive even. Keep quiet. Walk on. Softly – though already the snow muffled footsteps. I walked certainly, as if I'd done this before. All experience was narrowed to one point. This, it now seemed, had been my only purpose in Russia. To walk these streets with Captain S, through this very snow – who first and who following did not matter – and to meet him. I scanned the way for marks of the Captain's precise tread, but the snow was filling footprints as soon as they were made. I couldn't see even my own. The blank street behind me denied my existence.

I came into a quarter of broader streets, with snowy flower-beds in them and ornate lamps and big houses standing back that might be offices or ministries. A droshky waited at the kerb, the hunched driver scarcely distinguishable from his cab and horse – the three incorporated in one frozen object that shone where the snow had melted from it and was white where the snow still clung. Now that I identified this object – which because of the phantasmagoric snow had at first seemed fixed and natural, like a tree or a rock – I identified another in the distance where the street became blizzard. I couldn't judge whether it was moving. I threw a coin to the driver of the cab – it was a charm that brought him and his horse to life with a jerk – and waved him forward. Probably he was used to the wordless whims of men in a hurry. We didn't go fast – it was like nothing so much as being trundled through the storm in a large and shabby perambulator – but it was better than walking. The other cab I'd seen kept its lead. I was sure the Captain was in it. The two vehicles maintained this equal speed, my driver oblivious of my pantomime of urgency. The buildings we passed were unmistakably governmental; and we two wanted men were drawn slowly past the unseeing windows of the men who wanted us.

But now the first cab had stopped. It grew bigger to my view – and bigger still as it returned to pass us, empty, the two drivers raising their whips in ritual salute. The Captain had been put down somewhere. When I saw the place – for he stood outside to make sure I should see it – I felt he had cheated. It was a restaurant, approached by a path between pots of exotic flowers. The path had an awning. The doors were opened by flunkeys. I dismissed my cab and followed the Captain in.

In choosing this venue he put me at several disadvantages. He was at ease in such a place. I wasn't, and never had been. My territory was elsewhere. Besides, he was dressed for it, in elegant mufti. My private soldier's uniform attracted frowns. And there were graver disadvantages. He had lost his game already: by following him into this place I jeopardised mine. But I followed him. The bond between us was woven of too many threads to be broken casually. It demanded formal severance and sundering. Our tortuous relationship – like a piece of music, or anything else elaborate, unnecessary, yet, once existing, imperative – must be pursued to its proper close. There was no breaking it off short.

So I entered the restaurant, surrendered my coat – but not my gun – and followed a waiter, not heeding what was said to me, passing among people with an unconsciousness which probably was my best safe-conduct. I was led to a table near the Captain's. 'Champagne,' I said. They drank enough of it to know its native name. I'd not been in such a restaurant for a long time. I'd forgotten that such places existed. Just as the people sitting there had forgotten, if they ever knew it, the existence of that Russia I'd ridden through. No, I didn't think they'd ever known it, except by report. There were ancient staff officers sitting glum with their wives or gay with young women who might be ballet dancers. And there were loudly-talking, expensively dressed, over-jewelled men and women, several with children, of the kind who somehow always seize profit from the bankruptcy and collapse of nations. More French was being spoken than Russian. And there was Captain S.

He nodded to me, as if we had seen each other there every morning of our lives, as if we always nodded without caring to develop the acquaintance. Probably he wished we'd never done more than nod. But he came to my table and asked permission to join me. I shrugged assent. He sat and plucked nervously at a folded napkin and murmured, 'I shall be caught sooner or later, by one side or the other, in any case. Or killed in the further fighting that must come. But you can go free. Will you forfeit the rest of your life merely for the pleasure of terminating mine? You flatter me. We both have won and lost in our contest. There is no more to be won. Let me go. I don't go a pleasant way, if that's any satisfaction to you.'

'I daren't turn my back on you. You daren't turn yours on me. I ought to be able to kill you now – I'm armed and I think you're not – but some flaw in my education prevents it. Get a gun.'

We were speaking slowly, engraving our words again.

'You've been more lucky than clever,' he said. 'Even if my errors were part of your luck. Who would have expected that wretched girl to take your side?'

'She deserted yours rather than took mine. And you of all people should have expected that. You'd done it yourself. The prestige of the secret police has indeed swayed the people – swayed them to destroy it.'

'No. Only to change its master.' He spoke truth there.

'Get a gun,' I said.

'And if I refuse?'

'I shall give you up. It means giving myself up too. But the British authorities here will have me released. Nobody will intercede for you.'

He looked at me, and saw I meant it, and rose and walked across the restaurant. I followed, and you may believe that my hand was on my gun all the way. He spoke to the manager in the office, who produced a pistol that presumably was kept for use against thieves. The man showed no curiosity about the purpose it was wanted for. Possibly he was used to patrons settling disputes on the premises. Possibly he found it politic to show no curiosity. 'Extraordinary' was a word without meaning in Russia then.

Captain S led me into a garden behind the restaurant. A few tables indicated that people dined there in fine weather, but now we had it to ourselves. The lawn was white with snow, and the leaves of evergreens bore little piles of flakes. A broken figure of Cupid stood in the centre of the lawn – not native work, I thought, but imported to please the Francophile taste of fashionable clients – and seemed hopelessly to scan the snowy waste for a worthy mark. I wondered how it had been broken – whether in lover's rage or drunken revel or in a meeting like this.

We took our stations at opposite ends of the lawn, so that Cupid was poised between us but below our line of fire. I didn't watch the Captain's face. I watched his pistol hand. I had a sense of futility, cold and nauseous as the air.

I think there was a drinking-bowl in Cupid's pedestal, for a bird alighted there and tapped the ice vainly. 'When the bird flies away,' I said. We stood facing each other, bodies turned sideways to present the narrowest target, pistol arms outstretched. The Captain's pale clothes gave him a degree of camouflage in the snow. I held my front sight just below the darkness of his necktie.

The bird didn't give up easily. The muscle of my upper arm was beginning to ache because of the revolver's weight, and my hand to tremble. I had to keep blinking snowflakes from my eyes. Still the bird sought its water. Captain S suddenly dropped his arm, turned his back on me and walked away. I kept my sights on him. I knew his tricks. I still had my sights on his retreating figure when my arms were gripped from behind and I found myself standing among a party of British naval ratings.

The petty officer in charge of them addressed me by name. 'You'd better come with us,' he said. He was a fellow of about my age, but I felt much older. 'Sir,' he added uncertainly. The little Russian had declined to remain a passive spectator. I wasn't sure whether I was grateful or angry; and anyway he wasn't there to be thanked or upbraided.

'Who's that?' demanded the petty officer, indicating Captain S, who was still visible walking away between the farther hedges of the garden.

I stood watching him, and saw that he was pitiable – like each of us whose errands are never worthy of our powers and eventually reduce them. He had predicted once that I should fall into the hands of 'the others' – the Reds, I saw now he had meant – and afterwards become one of Russia's derelicts. Well, I'd escaped the first peril. But dereliction was a thing I might bring on myself without anybody's help; for I took its essence to be forgetfulness of purpose. My first purpose was to report in London. Anything else was incidental. The impetus of vengeance had been too often checked. Besides, he'd done me harm enough. If I caused his death – and his arrest would amount to that – he would hold my conscience with him in the grave. Already my remembrance had too many graves to visit.

'I don't know,' I said.

The petty officer looked at me sceptically, but his orders didn't go beyond rescuing me. The manager of the restaurant had appeared, holding one of the posters that advertised my escape. He pointed at me and cried 'Spy!'

'Spy, my foot,' said the petty officer. 'He's a deserter. We're taking him back to the ship.' To prove it he put handcuffs on me. The manager began to protest, but the fixed bayonets of the picket persuaded him he was mistaken. Instead he pointed after the Captain. 'That person has misappropriated my firearm,' he said. Obviously the British intervention in Archangel had prompted him to buy a phrase-book.

'Then I should get it back again if I were you,' said the

petty officer. And we left him doing that. He was the only man in Russia I had known take advice.

I said before that I could not read my future in the bright stars. So I could not expect to find in the grey side of the battleship or the grey waters of the sea any sign of how things would go for mc at home, any sign that much I banked on would fail and much else, unthought of, prosper. Looking back, I see a balance. Looking forward, on the quay at Archangel, I saw nothing. And anyway I had no leisure to read signs. A seaman stretched a hand to help me aboard. 'You've taken your time, mate,' he said.

All-action Fiction from Panther

*The author who 'makes Alistair Maclean look like a beginner' (*Sunday Express*)

†'The natural successor to Ian Fleming' (*Books & Bookmen*)

Bestselling British Fiction in Panther Books

GIRL, 20	Kingsley Amis	40p ☐
I WANT IT NOW	Kingsley Amis	35p ☐
THE GREEN MAN	Kingsley Amis	30p ☐
THE EXPERIMENT	Patrick Skene Catling	40p ☐
FREDDY HILL	Patrick Skene Catling	35p ☐
THE CATALOGUE	Patrick Skene Catling	35p ☐
THE SURROGATE	Patrick Skene Catling	45p ☐
THE EXTERMINATOR	Patrick Skene Catling	30p ☐
THE DECLINE OF THE WEST	David Caute	60p ☐
GEORGY GIRL	Margaret Forster	25p ☐
THE FRENCH LIEUTENANT'S WOMAN		
	John Fowles	50p ☐
MY FATHER IN HIS DIZZERBELL	Douglas Hayes	35p ☐
THE SHY YOUNG MAN	Douglas Hayes	40p ☐
THE WAR OF '39	Douglas Hayes	30p ☐
TOMORROW THE APRICOTS	Douglas Hayes	35p ☐
A PLAYER'S HIDE	Douglas Hayes	35p ☐
THE GOLDEN NOTEBOOK	Doris Lessing	90p ☐
BRIEFING FOR A DESCENT INTO HELL		
	Doris Lessing	40p ☐
A MAN AND TWO WOMEN	Doris Lessing	40p ☐
THE HABIT OF LOVING	Doris Lessing	50p ☐
FIVE	Doris Lessing	60p ☐
WINTER IN JULY	Doris Lessing	50p ☐
THE BLACK MADONNA	Doris Lessing	50p ☐

The Best Reading in Adult Fantasy and Horror Fiction is in Panther Books